KATY EVANS

BOSS

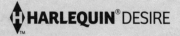

Recycling programs
for this product may
not exist in your area.

ISBN-13: 978-1-335-60350-0

Boss

Copyright © 2019 by Katy Evans

Printed in U.S.A.

www.Harlequin.com

One

My motto as a woman has always been simple: own every room you enter. This morning, when I walk into the offices of Cupid's Arrow, coffee in one hand and portfolio in the other, the click of my scarlet heels on the linoleum floor is sure to turn more than a few sleepy heads. My employees look up from their desks with nervous smiles. They know that on days like this I'm raring to go, and heads will roll if I don't get exactly what I want.

"Gather around the conference table, everyone. The morning brief begins in two minutes," I call out.

Ben, the head of the tech department who only attends important meetings of my design team, is the first to lurch toward me. He's got a coffee half extended, and he looks suddenly sheepish when he realizes I've already bought my own. His cheeks are flushed, clashing with his straw-colored hair.

"I didn't know if you'd have time to grab a coffee... but now you have two."

I smile at him as I put my things down on the conference table to accept his gift.

"Skinny latte."

"Your favorite." He shoots me a smile.

I take a sip and smile back. "Well, a person can never get too much coffee. Thank you."

"Anytime."

I take a long gulp from my foam cup, relishing the hot liquid. I can practically feel the caffeine entering my system and I'm so grateful. This will definitely be a long day, and I need all the boost I can get.

Today, I need things to go *perfectly*.

With everyone slowly filtering into their seats around the conference table, I take my position at the head and turn on the wall screen. The whole group looks up at me with wide eyes. *Watch and learn,* I think to myself, *this is how the professionals get things done, people.*

"All right, now that everyone's here, let's begin," I start. "As you all know, we've been focusing on revamping the brand. Can anybody tell me what I'm looking for in the new design?"

No one replies.

I sigh.

God. Sometimes I feel like I'm some sort of babysitter.

"Talk to me, Ellie, seeing as no one else will." I glance at my best friend since middle school, Ellie Mason. She followed me to Cupid's Arrow when I landed my dream job and needed to fill some vacancies on my team, and I've never regretted having both a best friend and a talented designer on board.

"The app's color scheme is fundamental to grasping the audience we want," she begins, her speech polished and thought out. "Cupid's Arrow is first and foremost a dating app for young people. It's possible they could be put off by the dark colors used on the home page and the messenger. What we need is a burst of color to attract the eye."

"Yes, Ellie. Thank God somebody's listening to me," I say, causing my other team members to laugh. "So, with that in mind, what has everyone come up with? Let me see."

My entire team scrabbles in their briefcases for the folders that should've been on the table five minutes ago.

"Seriously, guys?" I laugh in disbelief, then shoot them all a look that says they should know better.

Tim, the youngest member of my team, finally pulls out a design consisting of color blocking in primary colors. I bite the inside of my cheek as I review the idea.

"Tim, this is good…except the primary colors only appeal to children. This is a dating app. We don't really want seven-year-olds to start dating yet, do we?"

Tim laughs and looks a little embarrassed, and I smile kindly and give him a brief nod, trying to hide my exasperation. I glance at the rest of my team, hoping we've got something better, already feeling my nerves start to rattle. Alastair wants the color scheme decided on today, and to be honest, so do I. I take a quick look at everybody's work, pulling out the best ideas.

Not a lot is fabulous, unfortunately. Ellie has given me something good, though. She smiles as she passes me her portfolio with a look that tells me she prays we'll use hers. I don't smile back because I try never to play favorites—at least, not in the office.

After everyone has presented their ideas, I lay my own out for the others to inspect.

"It needs to be more like this," I tell them, clicking on the wall screen remote. I show them the hues of red and gray I've picked out. "Gender neutral. Striking. Denoting passion. Bold with lasting impact. It's timeless, something that everyone can be drawn to."

The team gazes with interest at the plans on the screen. It pains me to keep from telling them this is how they should've been doing it all along. Ellie can see the frustration on my face and she smirks, leaning back in her chair to enjoy my moment of annoyance.

I fix her with my best glare.

A whole morning has been wasted on something so easy.

Fantastic.

"Let's take Ellie's and my designs as a starting point and fine-tune the color scheme. Each of you will choose three by the end of the day so that we can whittle it down to a final idea. Is that clear?"

Everyone nods enthusiastically, reenergized by my presentation. As they all drift back to their desks to begin work, I pull a face at Ellie. It's a dark look to match my frustrated mood; my team always manages to wind me up on the most important days. Ellie points to my coffee.

"Feed the grump monster," she says with a grin.

Of course, my best friend knows caffeine is good for my soul.

I give her one last dirty look and finish off my second cup of the day. It's 10:00 a.m. and I'm already wiped out. At least I know the team will probably choose my design. Though it sounds bigheaded, I know my ideas are always the best. There's a reason Cupid's Arrow swept me up at age twenty. There's a reason I'm the head of the department after only four years—four years of unfailing enthusiasm, dedication and hard work. I carry the design team entirely on my own back, and I deserve recognition for it.

Ben walks over while I'm organizing my things.

"Thanks for coming, Ben. I suppose we don't really have anything decided yet, but I'll let you know as soon as we find our winning design so you can start working on your end."

"Of course," he says. "What are you doing after work tonight?"

I feel a little sad telling him that I plan to go home and reheat last night's Chinese takeout. It's a shame that I've always been a lousy cook because food is one of the highlights of my day. "I think I'll have a quiet night tonight," I tell him, as though I usually go out partying rather than slipping into pajamas and catching up on *Grey's Anatomy*.

"Forget that. We should—"

The office doors swing open to reveal Alastair Walker—the CEO of Cupid's Arrow, and the one person I answer to around here.

"How's the morning slug going, my dear Alexandra?" he asks in that British accent he hasn't quite been able to shake off, even after living in Chicago for a decade. He's adjusting his sharp suit as he saunters into the room. For his age, he's a particularly handsome man, his gray hair and the soft creases of his face doing little to steal the limelight from his tanned skin and toned body.

At the sight of him, Ben quickly eases back.

"The slug is moving sluggishly, you might say," I admit, smiling in greeting.

When Alastair walks in, everyone in the room stands up straighter. I'm glad my team knows how to behave themselves when the boss of the boss is around. But my own smile falters when I notice the tall dark-haired man falling into step beside Alastair.

A young man.

A very hot man.

One in a crisp charcoal suit, haphazardly knotted red tie and gorgeous designer shoes, with recklessly disheveled hair and scruff along his jaw.

Our gazes meet. My mouth dries up. I'm completely dazed all of a sudden. I've never seen a guy look so handsome or so cool without even trying.

He's got a head of dark brown curls.

Light brown, almost *amber* eyes.

The shadow of a beard across a square jaw.

A body to die for.

Tall. With shoulders a mile wide, perfectly hugged by his unbuttoned jacket.

I don't know what he's doing with Alastair, but I know he's the best-looking man I've *ever* seen in my life.

It's like the whole room shifted on its axis when he entered. And not only that, but it feels like somebody just tilted *my* axis a little bit to the left, a little bit to the right, and now, I can't seem to set it back to center.

"Everyone. I'd like to present my youngest son, the black sheep of the family." Alastair slaps the younger man on his back. The man's lips curve in amusement, but I notice that his eyes gleam in something like challenge over Alastair's black sheep comment.

A prick of empathy stabs me in the chest as I watch him step forward and finish for his father. "Kit Walker," he says, his voice deep and rich. His gaze pauses on me, and my chest constricts again as we stare.

"And this," Alastair tells him as he motions Kit forward, "is Cupid Arrow's secret weapon, Alexandra Croft."

Amber eyes hold mine and won't seem to let me go. *Breathe, Alex!*

Kit stretches out his hand. "A black sheep and a secret weapon. Sounds like a dangerous combination," he says in a low, teasing tone.

"Both easily underestimated," I add with a smile. I'm pleased that my voice is level as I extend my hand to shake his. His grip is warm, his eyes gleaming with curiosity and amusement—and *something else*. Something like respect.

He seems intrigued by my comment, aimed to let him know that I understand his frustration with his father. I don't think my parents expected me ever to get where I am.

"A pleasure to meet you, Kit," I say.

"The pleasure's mine." He speaks in a toe-curling British accent that should be outlawed in the States.

I realize we're both staring and pull my hand free, embarrassed my team saw me ogle him. I've heard stories about Alastair's youngest son. None of them good. Of course now that I see he has playboy looks to match his playboy reputation, I can believe that every single one of them is true.

"Well, why don't you all introduce yourselves to my son while I speak to Miss Croft?" Alastair tells the team. "Ben, we'll see you down in Tech later."

"Yes, sir," Ben instantly says.

Ben nods at Kit and Kit nods back, then my friend squeezes my arm in a gesture of comfort before he goes back to his floor.

Kit watches him disappear with a mild frown of curiosity on his face, then his gaze returns to me. It's inquisitive. Intense. I shake it off and briskly follow Alastair into his office.

Don't glance back, Alexandra. You've never allowed a guy to distract you and you aren't about to start now.

But I can't shake off the tingle in my hand, lingering from where Kit Walker touched me.

Two

Alastair opens the door to his office for us, gesturing for me to enter first. "Have a seat."

I straighten my suit jacket as I enter, suddenly a little nervous. I barely ever make room for nerves in my life. Usually, everything is on my own terms, and I can't help feeling relaxed that way. But this mysterious meeting has thrown me off. Suddenly, I'm paranoid that my job might be on the line.

Can it be?

Don't be silly, Alexandra, this place would crumble without you.

Alastair laughs at my expression as he crosses the room to sit behind his desk. "There's nothing to worry about, Alexandra. You know how much I value your contributions. Now please, sit down."

I'm awash with relief. I try and regain my composure, settling for a wan smile as I take a seat.

Alastair threads his fingers together and places them on top of his desk.

"This is hard for me to say. We've been colleagues for some time now, and you're one of my top employees. That's why I'm letting you know before the rest of the team—I'm leaving, Alex."

"What do you mean?" I sit up straighter, alarm shooting through me.

Alastair chuckles. "I thought you'd be pleased to see the back of me."

"Of course not!" I cry. How can my boss be leaving? Leaving where?

"I'm messing with you, Alex. Just teasing." Alastair watches me fondly, sipping the tea his assistant, John, brings to his desk.

"I don't know why you're so surprised. We all have to retire at some point. Even workaholics like you, eventually."

"Well, yes. But you're still…"

"Young?" Alastair finishes for me. He laughs again, shaking his head. "One of the things I love most about you is that you're so funny without meaning to be. Are you telling me you didn't see this coming?"

"Of course not. You didn't exactly give us any warning."

Alastair waves his hand dismissively. "Well. I'm telling you now. In fact, you're the first person to find out. I'm announcing my retirement officially at the end of the week."

I resist the urge to chew my nails, but I can't help feeling anxious. New management could change everything. I'm comfortable here in part because Alastair is British and has a laid-back management style. He moved here over two decades ago with his first wife, a wealthy American, and stayed here even after his divorce. He has been a very easy and kind boss. He basically gives me the run of my office. I'm able to do things my own way. If he leaves, what else will change?

"So what does this mean for us?" I ask. "And why are you telling me?"

"I'll get to that in a moment. I actually have a favor to ask."

"Anything you want," I tell him, and I mean it. Alastair made me what I am today. He took a chance on me, and I wouldn't have gotten this far without him. I will happily do anything he asks.

"I'm telling you first because you are responsible. I know you carry a lot of the workload, possibly more than me. I'm not embarrassed to say that I've had very little involvement in this company, because I'm lazy. It's true, you can't deny it. A bit of a womanizer, too. I started this business trying to bring dating into the information age. I never thought it would be the success it is now, top three in the field. It's a lot in part thanks to you, Alex."

My lips twitch a little. "That's okay. You've been a great boss. Two marriages, two divorces, two sons to look after, plus…well, you're charismatic. We can't deny your presence is required at every red carpet event ever thrown in this city."

Alastair laughs a little louder than necessary, slapping his hand down on his desk. "True, true. Well, I admit I've grown—my character has matured—along with this business. And I've always seen you as my little protégée I think you could help run this joint someday. But of course, there's someone else set to inherit by default."

I know he's speaking of his sons. I know his eldest is some hotshot at a media company and that Kit is the party boy, that he'd been off in Thailand or somewhere for three years.

"William's got his own empire to run," he begins, as if reading my mind. "And Kit...he was in Thailand for a while. But it's time he learned the meaning of hard work. Or at least work."

He leans back. "Kit has absolutely zero experience, but I don't see that as an issue, to be honest. When you came to me you were inexperienced as well, and look how far you've come? Kit..." He frowns as though considering how to phrase it. "The issue lies in his personality. He's not cut out for company life as of yet. Kit's just like his old dad at his age—lazy, unfocused, immature. It runs in our blood, I'm afraid. And his mother didn't do much to improve our bloodline, I might add."

Everyone knows Alastair married his second wife, some sort of stripper he met on a trip to London, only because she got pregnant with Kit. She was a party girl and Alastair gave her the boot pretty quick.

"But the thing is, Kit's still young. He's not set in his ways like me. I think with some guidance, he could be good at this whole thing. He seems keen on taking over, anyway."

Of course he is, I think to myself. Let's be honest, what guy wouldn't want to be in charge of a multibillion-dollar company with hundreds of employees?

"He's smart as a whip, Alex," my boss continues, eyebrows drawn as if sensing my reluctance. "He's cool as a cucumber, too. He could excel here. I'm determined that he'll be of some use. I couldn't bear it if he turned out to be a failure and brought shame to the family name. He has so much potential."

I chew on my lip to squash my growing discomfort. The idea of someone so inexperienced in charge of me doesn't appeal in the slightest. But what can I do? I need to suck it up and keep hustling, like I always do. This job is everything to me.

"So what can I do to help you feel more at ease with this…transition?" I ask him.

Alastair chuckles. "Straight down to business as always. Well, in truth, Kit could use a mentor, but he would never accept that. He doesn't like to be told what to do. While he gets settled, I'm still going to flit in and out to keep an eye on him. But I can't be around all the time. I want you to guide him."

Guide him.

Guide that hot, sexy, womanizing playboy who's about to start playing the boss? Worse than that…*my* boss? My stomach clutches at the prospect.

"Why so silent now, Alex? My little prodigy, always with something to say, has no words for me?" He raises his brows. "Remember, you just promised you'd do anything for me."

I sigh, quietly admitting with a smile, "I shot myself in the foot there, didn't I?"

"I suppose you did." He smiles back.

I swallow the lump of nerves in my throat. I know that I don't have a lot of choice but to comply. But I know boys like Kit. They're cocky. They probably did well at school, breezing through exams easily with minimum effort. They feel ready to take on the world, but they never want to put in the work because they're not used to it.

I'm radically different. Preferring studies to parties. My parents were workaholic perfectionists with little time for me, and it's in my DNA to be a workaholic perfectionist, too.

Work was, and still is, my parents' religion. To the point we talk by phone only on Christmas and birthdays—and mostly, about *work*. All I have is my little sister, Helena, whom I've endeavored to put through the best college thanks to—once again—my hard work. She's in her second semester at Stanford and she and I are both very proud of that.

My parents have always believed that hard workers aren't born that way, they are made. They've given Helena and me very little financial help since we finished high school. They think it's formative. But I think that Helena, who is smart as a whip and hopes for a career in technology, deserves the best college education, too.

That's why this job is so important to me. Accomplishing my own dreams is helping me give my sister the same opportunity with hers.

A man like Kit would never know a thing about sacrificing for someone else. *A boy*, who's clearly enjoyed the good life and all the pleasures to be had before work even came into the picture. Babysitting him sounds complicated and that's not what I studied so hard for. I just don't like this idea at *all*.

I don't have *time* for lazy boys!

Unless my job depends on it, of course.

"Well, what do you want me to do?" I ask Alastair in an effort to grant his last request.

"Just be a guide to him. Once he trusts you, he might see how hard you work and want to follow in your footsteps. Watch him, teach him and…report to me."

"What is it that you want me to report?"

"How he's doing. His inheritance will hang in the balance. I want to be sure my boy is deserving of it. And I'm hoping, to be honest, that with you as inspiration he will be even more adept at this than I am."

I clasp my fingers together tightly in my lap to contain my feeling of dread. I'd hate bearing the burden of being his son's new judge, but I love Cupid's Arrow too much to let it fall into the wrong hands, too. "And if my report is not…what you hoped it would be?" I ask.

"Then you help him change that. For the good of the company." After dropping that bomb on my lap, Alastair stands. "Let me call him in."

"Alastair, wait—" The idea of seeing Kit Walker again while I'm still getting my bearings doesn't sit too well with me yet.

Alastair is already at the door, summoning his play-boy son through his assistant. "John, call my son in, will you?"

I'm on my feet and within two minutes, there's a triple rap on the door. It's light and casual—and Kit doesn't even wait for Alastair to invite him in. The door swings open—and yes.

Alastair's youngest son is still the hottest man I've ever seen.

Alastair is back behind his desk. "Come in, Kit. Alex and I were just discussing you and Thailand."

Kit leans his shoulder against the doorframe and slides his gaze to me. "Of course you were," he croons in that soft British accent.

What's that supposed to mean?

"So, Alex," he says as he moves farther into the office and heads around his father's desk, "you ever been out of Chicago?"

"I go by Alexandra. Or Ms. Croft," I say all of a sudden, tipping my chin back haughtily.

Alastair laughs, and Kit raises his brows. "Ah well. *Miss* Croft," he murmurs, a playful twinkle in his eye. "Any other instructions for me before I take charge here behind this…very…desk?" He raps his knuckles on it and inspects it, pretending to be impressed as if he had never seen one before.

Is he making fun of me? Did he overhear us, or is it simply that he's smarter than he looks and knows what his father was up to from the beginning?

I bristle a little. Almost wanting to warn him. *Yes. Watch your back! This place is for people who value*

work and don't throw time away like you do your girls!
But I don't say that.

Still, emboldened by what Alastair has just requested of me, I say, "Only that your father has always trusted me to do what's best for my team—I expect the same courtesy from you, Mr. Walker."

"Oh. I go by Kit." His lips begin to curve upward. "And I'll do my best to grant you as much freedom as my father does, *Miss* Croft." He smiles completely now; a drop-dead gorgeous smile perfectly suited to that drop-dead gorgeous face.

I know he's playing with me. And I start to suspect there is more to this boy than just a pretty face—like Alastair said, he has intelligence, pride and obviously a keen sixth sense. And I can't help but feel my reaction to Kit's smile deep in my gut.

God help me. It's going to be a long day. A long month. Worse…a long year, if the bastard stays. I smile tightly in return and nod my head. "Well then, I'll be ready. Now, am I excused? Some of us need to get back to work." I try to say that playfully, though Alastair knows I'm a workaholic and rarely make room for chit-chat at work. He nods and I head out. Back straight, shoulders rigid, as if I'm not acutely aware of Kit Walker's eyes on me as I leave.

"Is he not the most gorgeous—" Angela, one of the most boisterous members of my design team, purrs the moment I reach my floor.

"Get back to work," I snap. Everyone looks up from what they're doing.

I head to my private office in the back and exhale, wondering why that sexy, coddled playboy pushed buttons I was never really aware of before. Until now.

Three

It's been a week since Alastair told me he was retiring, and now I'm sitting at my dresser, preparing for his retirement party. He's hired out a posh hotel on Michigan Avenue where over three hundred employees will gather to celebrate his time at Cupid's Arrow.

"I still can't believe how gorgeous Alastair's youngest is," Ellie says. "I can't believe Alastair asked you to help teach him the ropes."

I start brushing my hair and smirk at her. "Good genetics. Alastair is very good-looking, too. He has two sons from different marriages and a string of affairs to attest to how those Walker men are candy to the ladies."

I twist my hair back into a bun as quickly as possible so that I can finish my makeup. I may be a designer, but styling hair has never been my strong point. I continue with my makeup, ensuring that it enhances my blue-green eyes and light skin tone.

Why am I so nervous about tonight?

Is it because Alastair is leaving…or because *Kit* is taking over?

"I'm sort of dreading this whole thing, Ellie. I mean… Why does Alastair think I have the ability to change some playboy into a model boss and entrepreneur? It's ludicrous, really."

"But you *did* notice the way you two sort of lit up the whole room when you saw each other?" Ellie, not one to miss anything, asks.

A little tingle races down my spine at the thought of seeing Kit again.

I try to push the memory of our initial meeting aside, but the nervousness increases. I examine my face and figure in the mirror, wanting to look perfect.

My hours at the gym have paid off and my slinkiest black dress finally fits me again. It hugs my hips and shows off the perpetual flatness of my chest and stomach. It makes me look professional, at least, and that's what I need this evening.

I spritz some perfume on my neck and wrists. "No, I won't admit to that," I finally say in my effort to put that meeting past me. "In fact, I think you're seeing things, and I blame your new low-carb diet." Fixing my hair one last time in the mirror, I quickly change the subject. "Okay, I'm ready. You?"

I cross the room to find a suitable pair of shoes while Ellie takes my place on the vanity bench. "I'm ready. But are we seriously not going to talk about this? Alex, we've been friends for ages. Even before Cupid's Arrow. We grew up together. I *know* you."

"Okay, fine. I haven't been on a date in two years and I suppose I was struck by the man's utter beauty and his gorgeous—we can't deny it—British accent," I say, slipping on my favorite red heels. "That speaks volumes about me, don't you think? That some stranger can just throw me off the way he did?"

Ellie laughs. "It speaks volumes that you need to get *laid*. Even workaholics need a little playtime."

"Not this one. And especially not with him. God, he was such an ass in Alastair's office, Ellie!" I stand up, wriggling my toes in my shoes to make sure they're comfortable enough to drive in. "I suppose if a decent man asked me on a date, maybe I'd go out with him."

This week I've been sleepless, wondering why meeting Kit has made me think a lot about the romance in my life—or lack thereof. And how much I'd love to change that.

"Like who?"

I shrug. "I don't know."

Ellie arranges her bun and twirls around, inspecting herself in the mirror. "Yeah, well. I do. Alastair's son. You would totally date him."

"No, I shouldn't. Alastair once told me his eldest son, William, is like his first wife, who was very responsible and divorced Alastair because he was such a mess in his younger years. But if Kit is anything like his father when he was younger or that stripper second wife he married, I wouldn't touch him with a ten-foot pole. Players aren't my thing."

Ellie frowns at me, looking disappointed.

I laugh. "I just like guys that aren't complete ass-
holes, Ellie. Like that one boyfriend who was so easygoing. Maybe *too* easygoing to the point maybe I thought
he didn't care?" I grab my car keys from my dresser
and pull Ellie to the door. "I know what you're thinking. But I'm not picky. I just have standards."

Ellie and I head out to the car together, compliment-
ing each other's outfits.

"I have standards, too, but I occasionally date, you
know?" she counters as we get in my car. "It's not a bad
thing to recognize that you're a woman and have needs."

I groan and playfully swat her shoulder before starting the engine. "Stop it. I need to be professional tonight
and I can't be moping around about my datelessness
these past two years."

The truth is that I'm more nervous than I'm letting
on.

I haven't been to a party in a while, let alone one
as important as this. Kit will be there tonight. I need
to make the right impression from the start. Do I act
professional? Do I try to be friendly with him in a way
that's totally out of character for me? I'm not sure what
Alastair will expect.

"Are you going to pull out of the parking spot?"

I blink, realizing I've been sitting in the driver's seat
for a solid minute. I shake my head at myself, shifting
into Drive.

"Wow. Alex Croft, completely dazed by a guy." Ellie
laughs.

As I pull into traffic, I rub at my eye absentmindedly,

then quickly pray I haven't smudged my makeup. "This has nothing to do with *a guy*. We barely exchanged words. It's just that tonight is important."

"I've never seen you so flustered. Do you want to talk about it?"

"No," I say bluntly. Then I laugh when she just wags her eyebrows. "You know I'm nervous about this whole deal. Me babysitting that…player. I'm nervous that after Alastair gives his goodbye speech later tonight, there'll be no turning back and we'll all have Kit Walker as a boss."

Ellie sighs dreamily. "Another reason to wake up with a smile in the morning. Just to see him in the office—"

"Ellie!" I groan, part of me wishing I could be so carefree about men and dating like she is.

When we park outside the hotel, I grab my handbag from the backseat and spend a minute fixing myself up in my wing mirror. Ellie does the same.

"Speaking of possible dates…look who's here just in time. Methinks some guy at the office likes you."

As I peer out the window, I spot Ben walking toward us. "Hey, Alex. You look great." He opens the door for me.

"I—ah, thanks Ben."

"No, really, you do. You sound like you don't believe me."

"I, uh, no, I'm…"

"Ben, she knows she looks hot."

He frowns at Ellie, then shoots me this sad little smile. It's probably the kind of look that normally has girls swooning at his feet. He's got a certain charm, that one. Not that it appeals to me much. He's a friend, and that's how I want it to stay.

"Okay then," he says absentmindedly. As I straighten up, he offers me his arm and I take it, letting him lead Ellie and me inside the hotel.

The party is already getting going, even though it's early.

Alastair has always known how to throw the best parties. The music and decor are just right: young, simple but edgy. When the guests are happy, everything is good. I just wish I could get in the spirit of it.

"Alastair knows how to get the best vibe. I'll miss his parties," Ben says, staring around in awe as Ellie goes over to talk with Angela.

A waiter passes by with glasses of champagne and Ben thanks him as he accepts a glass. The waiter offers me one with a smile and I shake my head, though a drink would really calm my nerves right now.

But I've always told myself that I'm not one of those people who need a drink to feel confident.

I guess I'm regretting that stance now.

"Where's Kit? Have you seen him?" I ask Ben. He wrinkles his nose, half his glass already poured down his throat.

"Who cares? I'm sure you'll see him later. We should be having fun."

"It's a staff party. It's not meant to be fun."

"Everyone else is having a good time," Ben points out. He gestures over to Tim, who has a girl from Accounting on his arm and three empty glasses of champagne on the table beside him. I sigh.

"I can't cut loose. Not tonight."

"Suit yourself," Ben says, finishing off his glass. "Are you coming with me?"

He points to the bar and I shake my head. "I'll wait here awhile."

Ben shrugs and wanders off alone, grabbing another glass of champagne as he saunters into the thick of the party. I curse myself for being no fun, but tonight is about business for me. I have to be ready.

I spot Ellie chatting with the other girls and smile at her, motioning that I'll be right over. I make a trip to the bathroom and when I emerge, male voices coming from a nook down the hall catch my attention.

British-accented voices.

"…hope you act responsible for once like your brother. I'm asking Alexandra to take you on and report to me as you learn the ropes and that's that."

"I don't need to be taken on by your favorite pet. I know a thing or two about business."

"Right. Dropping out of college to travel around the world taught you all the ropes?"

"Gut instinct. Believe me, Pops, you can learn things out in the streets that you can't learn in a classroom."

"Well all I know is this is the only chance you're getting, Kit. Your brother already has a—"

"I know William made it big on his own. I never asked for this company. You want me here. Face it."

"True. So show me I wasn't wrong."

"You're not wrong, but I appreciate you letting me

bring my own cards to the table and not stepping on my toes."

I ease away when the voices sound closer and hurry back into the ballroom.

And seriously?

Ouch.

I'm smarting over being called *pet*. I'm not Alastair's *pet*. I like pleasing my boss. Hell, I *need* this job. It's not my fault Kit has it all on a silver platter and doesn't want someone like me looking over his shoulder and reporting back to his dad. I'm fuming and feeling irritated at the guy. It also irks me that he's young and that he's handsome, and that for a moment there, on the day we met, I was interested in him in a way I haven't been interested in a man in a long time. I *felt* something. A connection.

Stupid Alex.

I shake my head at myself, then scan the room for Ellie. There's sudden loud applause coming from the main ballroom. Alastair must be about to make his speech. Trying to forget what I just heard, I enter the room and push through the crowd to get a good spot at the front. This speech matters to me more than I want to let on. I'll be sad to see Alastair go.

When I reach the stage, the applause is dying down and Alastair is standing with a microphone, looking casually cool and collected as usual. As if the conversation between him and his youngest son was nothing out of the ordinary.

"Good evening, everyone. Welcome to my retirement party. I know you're all thrilled to see me go, and

I see some of you are already celebrating so much you won't remember this whole evening even happened."

There are laughs and cheers from the corner of the room. I suspect it's Tim and Ben in their semidrunken state, but I'm praying for the sake of our department's reputation that it's someone else.

"Now before I get far too drunk myself—" Alastair pauses amid another smattering of laughter "—I'd like to say some thank-yous."

I scan the room to see if I can spot Kit but the crowd is too thick to see much of anything.

"Thanks to my trusted friend and finance manager, Erin Gough," Alastair is saying, "To Ben, on the technical side of things. We'd trip up without you, Benny! And I'd especially like to thank my design team. For an app like Cupid's Arrow, you need a vision, and my most faithful employee helped me bring my idea to life." He finally spots me in the crowd and fixes me with his amber eyes, so much like Kit's. "Thank you endlessly, Alexandra Croft, for working far too hard to make my dream a reality."

I blush as the crowd applauds. I've always known that Alastair holds me in high regard, but it's nice to hear his appreciation. He winks at me as he sets his microphone back on the stand, then picks it back up. It can only mean he's about to introduce his son. Nerves seize me again as I remember Kit's amber eyes and the connection I felt between us when we met, but I have to keep cool. This isn't *like* me. Not at all.

"Now, despite my retirement, I do plan to pop in from time to time to observe how my company is doing.

There will, of course, be new management, and it's my great honor to introduce my successor tonight. I hope that he can do me proud as we enter a new era at Cupid's Arrow."

This is it. Here he comes.

"Please give a warm welcome to my pride and joy, my son, Kit Walker!"

Loud applause erupts around me, but my senses are engulfed by the man taking the stage.

Four

I can't believe it, but my nipples actually prick when Kit steps up to the microphone. Is it possible that he's even more handsome than I remember? His hair is standing up, going this way and that, his tie knotted loosely in the collar of his shirt with its top button undone.

He starts speaking in that lovely British accent. I try not to get sucked in by the deep timbre of his voice.

If I've learned one thing in the years I've worked as a designer it's that good product design is like a good man. Both are rare.

It's almost impossible to find a design good enough to compliment a good product, and it's even harder to find a product good enough to match a good design. And the same goes for men: personality and good looks rarely go hand in hand, and I'm sure that Kit Walker is no exception to that rule.

It's such a shame when the contents don't match the packaging.

"When I told my father I was ready to get down to business," Kit is saying, "he asked me, what business?" There's laughter. "Because you see, Cupid's Arrow is more like love than work to my father. This company has always been more like his family. It's enough to make me jealous."

He's cool and casual and upbeat as he teases the crowd, acting like he'd just gotten an award for being the world's most clever schoolboy or something. I can tell that he's cocky and full of himself and I suddenly resent that. I also resent how the crowd is calling out to him from the sidelines, every employee thinking he can be chums with the new boss. Good grief. This guy has done absolutely nothing to earn his position. He hasn't even worked a day at Cupid's Arrow yet and everybody already loves him.

Or pretends to.

"Are you impressed by your team at Cupid's Arrow, Kit?" one of the rowdier men calls out.

"Well, I have to say, I can't wait to work with such a beautiful bunch of people," Kit replies breez- ily, his attention finally falling on Erin from account- ing, who's been waving from the sidelines as if she'll die if he doesn't personally say hello to her very soon. She blushes when he finally acknowledges her with a smile and I'm embarrassed on her behalf. I really am. I wouldn't like to be swooning so openly in front of him.

But then I feel myself blush, thinking that maybe, when we met, I was wearing a besotted look just like Erin is.

"I must admit, inheriting Cupid's Arrow represents a lot of firsts for me. And, well…the first time I rode a bike, I got a scar to prove it. I may make mistakes…" He pauses and looks at me then, as if all this time, he's known exactly—*exactly*—where I've been standing in the crowd. Then in a lower voice, he goes on. "In fact, most assuredly I *will* make mistakes, but at the end of the day, I plan to get it right. I will bring Cupid's Arrow into the new era with better service, a catchier design, a better slogan… Everyone into online dating and even those who aren't will be using our app."

This gets loud applause.

I can't believe my new boss has got them all in an uproar. He's never had a job in his life, and now he's heading one of the largest companies in Chicago. As someone who has had a job ever since I was sixteen, it's a bitter pill to swallow.

And I keep remembering how he looked at me when he talked about making mistakes, and I wonder why Alastair had to tell him I'd be his damn spy. Bloody hell, as these Brits would say.

Knotting up in discomfort, I feel a hand on my shoulder and turn around. Ben is behind me, his eyes half glazed in drunkenness and a smug smile on his lips.

"He seems to look forward to working with you," he whispers. His breath stinks of alcohol. I turn my face away in annoyance.

"I need a little air," I breathe, wanting to collect myself. I turn.

"Leaving so soon, Miss Croft?"

I turn back and Kit has his eyes fixed on me. He brushes his hair back from his face and though the move is casual, his gaze is anything but. The challenging gleam pins me in place.

Feeling defensive, I glare at him as he smiles slowly, raising an eyebrow at me.

"The party's only just getting started," he says as everyone watches. "Stay and play."

His eyes slide to Ben, then back to me. I inhale nervously. Kit stares at me like he owns me. Well, I can stare back for as long as he wants to keep up this little charade. All night if I have to. He won't get the better of me.

Kit's grin only grows wider.

He pulls the microphone stand with him like a practiced stand-up comedian, his gait relaxed as he heads from center stage to his left. Now we're directly opposite one another and only yards apart. Somehow, this power play is the most exciting part of the evening so far.

"Everyone," he says softly, his lips close to the microphone. "It's the woman of the hour, Alexandra Croft. I've heard a lot about you."

The way he says it makes me feel complimented and at the same time, exposed. Because his words make me flush. And my whole team can see it. I swallow, torn between glaring and turning away and meeting his gaze and demanding what it is he thinks he's doing. What else has Alastair been saying about me to Kit?

Kit sits down at the front of the stage, his legs dangling over the edge. He smiles, his breathing magnified by the microphone.

"I hope you enjoy this party, Alex," he says, a gleam in his whiskey eyes. "And I look forward to working with you as I...*learn the ropes*. Three cheers for Ms. Croft, everyone."

There's scattered applause again, but this time I sense a shift in the mood. No one could miss the tension between Kit and me. He smiles at me one last time before standing up and moving back to center stage.

"I think you've heard enough from me for now, folks. Let's get wasted, yeah?"

I think everyone in the room cheers but me. I think everyone here likes Kit but me. I think everyone here is blind but me. Those amber eyes and all those sexy smiles don't fool me one bit. I've seen beneath the surface, and I don't like what's there. Suddenly I want to be anywhere but here. Anywhere where that cocky kid isn't sharing my oxygen.

I head to the bathroom and splash my face with water, not caring when my mascara dribbles down my cheeks. Kit has wound me up so tight that I feel like anything could happen.

I went from dreaming of kissing him all week to wanting to knock him off his high horse. He's good. He's got everyone wrapped around his little finger. He's got women laughing at jokes at their expense. Because every woman loves a bad boy, right? Well, not me.

After I redo my makeup, I go back into the hall, hoping to find Ellie so that we can head home. Instead

I spot Ben, Alastair and Tim at the bar. I head over. "Alastair, can we talk?"

Alastair nods and draws me closer, guiding me to stand near an unoccupied table nearby. "Aren't you having a good time?"

"In all honesty? No, I'm not. I'm…concerned about this whole thing. Does your son know that I'm supposed to report his…progress to you?"

I know the answer, but I can't very well admit to overhearing their conversation, can I?

Alastair puts a hand on my arm, looking into my eyes. "Of course, Alex. He's my boy, he needs to know that I'm going to be watching his every move. Why? You're not going to quit on me now, are you?" He teases, a light smile on his lips.

"I am *not* a quitter," I promise. "But I also feel uncomfortable being put up against my new boss like that."

Alastair's face softens. "Of course you do, Alex. But don't look at it that way. That's the mistake he's making, too. You're on the same team. Why do you think I asked you to get involved? You can help that boy."

I shake my head in anger. "No. I really don't know that I can help him at all or that he wants my help."

"Ah. You're just backing away from a challenge." Alastair steps away from me coolly. "I thought you were better than that, Alex."

"Alastair, I'm not sure this is something I can do. I don't know if I can work with someone who may not take work as seriously as I do and I'm not sure…" I trail off.

That I can get along with your son, seeing the hostile gleam in his eyes.

I went from being the girl who could relate to him on our first introduction to his enemy in the space of a week. I hate that that happened and hate that I feel physically drawn to him regardless of the wall that's now gone up between us.

Alastair sighs, removing a key card from the dozens of keys he has in his pocket. "If you need a breather, go up to the suite I've rented and think this over. You'll have the place to yourself. I know you'll feel differently in an hour or so."

"I won't. Please ask someone else, Alastair," I beg.

"Your stubbornness will be your downfall, Alex." Alastair sighs and for the first time, I see a tiredness in his expression that's never been there before. "Do you think I wanted to see my youngest son turn out like this? I'm asking you to help me. As an old friend. If you don't think you can do that, then I guess you're not the person I thought you were."

Alastair leaves the key card on the table and walks away. I'm left alone in a sea of people enjoying the night. I long to walk straight out the door and head home. But Alastair's right. I'm not a quitter. I can't let some reckless British trust funder ruin my career. I snatch up the key card and head up to Alastair's hotel room to settle my mood.

Five

It turns out to be the penthouse. I guess it's not surprising that Alastair has the best spot in the hotel. And it's nice that he's given me sole access, but I'm still not happy with him. No amount of fancy four-poster beds and fur rugs can make me feel better about the task he's given me. Not even the panoramic view of Chicago can dredge a smile out of me tonight.

I lie back on the soft duvet, exhausted all of a sudden. I close my eyes, trying to block out my annoyance.

This job matters to me more than anything. I don't want it to be tainted by Kit's attitude. I wish things could just stay the same, but I guess like everyone else, I have to adapt to change.

I decide I need to stalk the guy a little, which is something I never do. But all I know about Kit so far is that I have no idea what to make of him. He's a wild card, and I don't like wild cards. I sort of hate him now, and hate that I'm attracted to him even more. It's not a good start, to say the least.

I check him out on social media, scrolling through his profiles on my phone. He's well connected, to say the least. He's on every platform imaginable, and he's not the kind to keep his profiles strictly friends and family. He's racked up tens of thousands of followers. I grit my teeth, trying to look for positives.

It's almost impossible. The more I look at his posts, the angrier I get. In every photo, Kit's got at least two scantily clad girls on his arms, looking up at him dotingly, like they just won the lottery because he decided to give them a few moments of his time.

He follows only a handful of people back, including a bunch of models. I roll my eyes, setting my phone aside. Stalking him has only given me more reason to dislike him. And I can't shake the memory of his amber eyes on mine. The challenge there. And something else I can't figure out.

I swing my legs off the bed and pad over to the mini-fridge. Inside, there are bottles of rosé, plus some miniature shot-sized vodkas. My hand hovers over them. Tonight has broken every rule in my book—starting when I let myself be pitted against my new boss by his own father. I take one of the vodka bottles and drink it straight before I can change my mind. Then I head back downstairs before I can give myself any more reason to back out.

The party is even more crowded than before. I spot

Ellie on the dance floor with Tim, and consider heading over. It would be such a relief to confess my worry over taking Kit on, but I don't want to spoil her night with my whining so I turn my attention away.

As the vodka seeps through my system, I'm finding it increasingly hard to see. I scan the room looking for Kit. There's no sign of him but I see his father. Then I spot an exit sign toward the back of the room. The door is slightly ajar. I head straight for it, needing a breath of fresh air.

It leads out to a parking lot behind the hotel. I'm not even slightly surprised when I spot Kit. There's a woman I don't recognize sitting on the hood of a car in the lot. They're talking, heads close together. I watch him lean down, and I wonder if they're about to kiss. He doesn't kiss her, though. I realize he was reaching for his phone behind her on the hood. He tucks it into his back pocket while she tips her head back, reaching out to stroke her fingers up his arm. She giggles as if he whispered something intimate in her ear.

Coming out here was a mistake. I'm about to head back inside when the girl spots me. She points and Kit turns around. The moment our eyes lock, my stomach does a backflip.

The girl slides off the car and pulls herself up beside him, taking his arm to try to attract his attention.

Kit doesn't seem to notice. He says something to her and she scampers past me back inside. He probably promised to look her up later, and the thought makes me a little madder.

My heart starts pounding as he heads over to me.

Our eyes hold and lock. I stand my ground, waiting until he's mere inches away from me. I need to crane my neck back a little to meet him eye to eye.

I'm five-four, but Kit is over six feet tall.

"Having a good evening, Miss Croft?"

"It certainly looks like you're getting to the *good* parts quickly."

Kit laughs, fishing in his blazer for a cigarette. "Do you smoke?"

"Absolutely not."

To my surprise, Kit puts the cigarette back in his pocket. "Cool. I keep them around to offer people. It seems polite, you know?"

I squirm. I wasn't expecting such pleasantries from him. What is it with these British guys and their unshakeable politeness? I search for that challenging gleam in his eyes from earlier, but see only curiosity instead. "What, so giving people lung cancer is polite now?" I ask.

Kit's smile falters a little. He frowns, as if confused about me. "Did you need something?"

"I came outside for some fresh air." But I'm finding it harder to breathe out here with Kit than inside in the crowd. Kit slides his hands into his pockets casually and leans against the wall of the building. His amber eyes hold mine in a gentle but firm lock and I pray he hasn't noticed how nervous I am.

I sense we're both thinking of the conversation I just overheard. I wonder if that's the sole reason I'm nervous.

"Do you really think you can keep me in line, Miss

Croft?" he asks, startling me. I'm surprised he's not crooning those words in an evil tone, but simply asking a question as if confused that I would even try.

"It's not my fault your father wants to keep an eye on you."

"I've never held an actual job before. That concerns him," he says easily, as though it's a normal thing to admit. "But the way my dad described you, I just thought you'd be…"

I cross my arms. "Yes?"

"Well, different."

"Different how?"

"I thought you'd be boring." He smirks at me with a devilish twinkle in his eyes. "But you're not. In fact, I think the words to describe you would be interesting, amusing. Stunning."

My cheeks burn. Not in embarrassment, and not because I'm swooning for this jerk. More because I'm angry that he thinks he can talk to me like that.

"We barely know each other," I say sharply.

Kit feigns surprise. "Oh, I'm sorry. Did I offend you with my compliment?"

"I'd say it's a backhanded compliment, actually."

He shakes his head. "Well, I never intended to hurt your feelings."

I tut at him. "You've got a lot to learn. You shouldn't speak to your colleagues like that."

"Like what?"

I flare up. "Like they're all your playthings. Don't call me stunning and think I don't know what you're doing. It might work on that girl you were just…just… *flirting with*, but not me."

"She's having more fun tonight than you are," Kit says, as though he's formed a well-constructed argument instead of another inadvertent insult.

"You're infuriating."

Kit smiles at me. "Not to everyone. I just know how to wind you up. I can read you like a book."

I take a deep breath, smoothing down my suit. "Look, Mr. Walker…"

"Kit," he corrects.

"Kit." I say his name, feeling a warm flush crawl up my neck as I speak it out loud. It feels intimate as I speak it, with nobody to hear it except me and him.

A devilish smile curves Kit's lips. I can tell he's thinking once more of what an open book I am.

"Look, Kit," I repeat, feeling my cheeks flush and my body tingle at his nearness. "We don't have to be friends, I just have to be civil. I don't like that I'm reporting on you to your father but he's asked me to, and because he's been so good to me and is still the owner, I agreed. It's nothing personal against you. He said I shouldn't look at you as an enemy and that we should— work together, to make this transition go smoothly. Is that clear?"

The amused sparkle in Kit's eyes steadily diminishes as I speak. He opens the door for me to go back inside. "Crystal clear, Ms. Croft. I look forward to *learning the ropes*," he says.

"Nothing would give me more pleasure than teaching you," I say primly, ignoring the sarcasm lacing his words.

As I pivot to pass him, I accidentally bump into his rock-hard shoulder. It makes me blush, as if I'm one of those swooning girls on his Instagram, but I refuse to look back even though I can feel Kit watching me as I go.

I chide my body to *get a grip, please*. If this is how I feel now, I dread what working with Kit Walker will be like tomorrow. He makes my thoughts scatter, and I don't like that.

He makes work seem like play and I take work seriously—I don't like that.

He makes me feel insecure compared to his cool, charismatic personality and I don't like that.

Most especially, he makes me wonder what it's like to be the kind of girl that sits on the hood of a car, flirting with a guy she likes while he flirts back.

Shaking aside the feeling of loneliness that suddenly fills me, I remind myself I'll brave this. I'm Alexandra Croft, that's what I do.

Six

I'm a little smug and not the least surprised when everyone at work is hung over except me the next morning. I'm fresh as a daisy, in fact.

After coffee and a croissant, I went to the gym before heading to the office. I arrived early and watched my colleagues dribble in like snails, looking as though they might collapse from fatigue.

"I heard people talking about last night," Ellie says, approaching me before our morning meeting. I shake my head and turn away to log on to my computer. "Something about Kit and a woman in the parking lot."

"They weren't doing anything but talking, even though she obviously hoped for more," I tell her.

She perches on the edge of her desk.

"Oh really? Well people think it was you and him, actually. They saw you two talking outside."

I almost gasp at that. I've always looked down on fraternizing in the office. It's just not good for anyone involved, and I would *never* be party to it.

I realize everyone is watching us. They're all craning their necks, trying to listen in on our conversation. I fight off a blush. I can't believe I've been mixed up with some little nobody from who knows where, one of Kit Walker's floozies.

"That wasn't me. And if whoever is saying that wants to keep his or her job, I suggest they stop spreading slander," I say loudly. I look over at Angela and her face falls. I'm not messing around here and she knows it. She's usually the most talkative of the team and I suspect she's the one who began the rumor in the first place.

"I just—" Angela begins.

"I don't care how fun it is to gossip about the new boss. If I hear anyone disrespecting him like that again, you'll have me to answer to. You would never speak that way about Alastair, and Kit deserves the same respect. Anyone who feels differently will be having a very serious conversation with me about their place in this company. Is that clear?"

Everyone nods silently, the buzz from last night's antics completely ruined. But I don't care. I won't have people talking about me that way. Kit might be happy to tarnish his reputation time and time again, but I am *not*.

I stand up, ready to deal with anyone else who thinks last night was a joke.

"Am I the only one around here interested in the fact that our app design needs to be finalized by next Friday? That's just a week, and the new boss is coming in today expecting to see what we've got so far."

The members of my team mumble halfhearted replies and robotically shuffle to their workstations. It angers me even more to see them so put off by the idea of hard work. I slam my hand against my desk and they all jump as though I've given them a new lease on life in their zombie-like state.

"All right, this isn't good enough. None of you are fit to be here. I won't allow my team to show up in a state like this. I want you all to go home. Now. I'll see you on Monday morning for a much-needed regroup. Get some rest, hydrate. And bring me your absolute *best* on Monday."

I figure it's unlikely Kit will even show up to work, considering everyone seems to have had too much to drink last night. I doubt Kit's ever woken up before noon a day in his life.

People rise from their seats, collecting their things in a daze. One by one, they filter out in silence. I'm about to sit back down when I notice Ben hanging out by the door, listening to everything.

He looks surprised when I spot him. His eyes are red and raw, and he's sporting a bruise on his forehead that he's tried to hide beneath his hair. But I can see right through his pale blond bangs.

"And what exactly happened to you?" I ask with a laugh, raising an eyebrow as he slumps into a vacant chair. He groans, leaning his forehead against a computer keyboard.

"Nothing," he says without conviction.

"Come on. Spill."

He sighs dramatically. "I fell over challenging Tim to handstands."

"Don't blame me!" Tim squeaks as he walks past the door, also looking worse for wear as he leaves. "You brought that on yourself."

"Well, I still expect that you'll be in top form Monday, Tim. Concussion or not," I say cheerfully. "And you, Ben? You know better."

"It's not that bad…" Ben claims moodily, rubbing at the sore spot on his head. "But you're right. There's no excuse for unproductive behavior." Ben salutes me sarcastically. "I can't leave for the day since I have my own team to manage, but now that you have some peace and quiet, I hope you have a good one."

"You too." I nod and turn to my desk while Ellie comes and kisses my cheek.

"Thank you, you're the best boss."

I groan. "Get out of here, Ellie, and please don't put me on the spot on Monday."

"I won't! Promise!" She heads out. But Ben is still lingering by the door.

He looks like he wants to say something, but he keeps his mouth shut. Without another word, he turns and leaves me alone with my thoughts in an empty office.

I work alone for most of the day. It's good to have the office to myself. I play some quiet music on my speakers and revel in the fact that there's no general chitchat in the background to distract me.

Sometimes, it's nice just to be on my own.

As the day passes, I gradually calm down. I convince myself that office rumors are just a fact of life. It's nothing personal toward me. In fact, I'm sure that whoever spread the rumor wasn't intending to be malicious, but just indulging in a little girly gossip. For her, hooking up with the hot new boss would be seen as a triumph. For me, though, I can't stand the thought.

Maybe it's because Kit is a one-way ticket to heartbreak and ruining the reputation I've worked so hard to earn for myself. Being seen as a no-nonsense woman who can get ahead by skills and merit rather than sleeping my way to the top is important to me.

Either way, I don't want inappropriate things being said about me behind my back. I want to make it clear to everyone that I wasn't that girl and that their new boss deserves as much respect as Alastair.

I remember our conversation in the parking lot and have to admit, there's something about him. I can't get him off my mind.

It's three o'clock and I'm still dazed when Kit bursts into the office. He's wearing a perfectly cut gray suit, and is so handsome he hurts my eyes. I sit up a little taller.

"Good afternoon, Ms. Croft."

"Hi," I say, concentrating on my computer screen even though I haven't typed anything in half an hour.

Suddenly the air feels charged. It's magnetic. Pulsing.

Kit slowly paces the room, looking around in confusion.

"Well, its not as lively as I expected…where's the rest of your team?"

"I…" I hesitate, my stomach in knots. I never once thought that Kit would actually show up at work today. "I sent them home for the day."

Kit frowns at me. I want to cringe at his annoyance. But business has taught me that once a decision is made, you have to stand firm.

There's a wry expression on his face. "And why did you send them home?"

"They weren't in any fit state to work, and I gave them time to regroup."

"You can't just send employees home, Alexandra."

I swallow. Alastair never put me on the spot like this. "I—I did."

"That's *my* job."

I grit my teeth for a moment and then look up at Kit, forcing a smile. "Your father taught me that I control my team. He never interfered—"

Kit snorts. "Huh. That's what my father told you?"

"That's what he *taught* me."

Kit's arrogant smile makes me want to slap him, but I sit still, glaring back at him. "Well, my father isn't here now. I'm in charge. Bring them all back in."

My eyes widen. "Work finishes in two hours. I'm not going to drag them all in from different parts of the city. They're useless today anyway. They let me down and I don't want us to turn in something sloppy."

"I'll decide if they're useless. Get in here."

I lean back in my chair, shocked but stubborn.

Kit's anger grows. His cheeks are flushed and his

smug smile is fading by the second. "Did you not hear me, or are you simply playing deaf, Ms. Croft?"

I shake my head. "I made a call on what to do and though you may not like it, I need to stick by it. This is my team and usually—"

"Your team works for me. In *my* office, in *my* building."

"I'm sorry if you don't like the way I run my team." I bristle. "Tell your father if you want, but I did what I thought was best. I apologize for the inconvenience to you, but they'll be back top-notch on Monday."

Kit is furious now. I can tell by the creases in his forehead, his pursed lips, his hands curled into fists. Well, take *that,* Kit. Now you know how it feels.

"You're walking a dangerous line, Alexandra." His voice is deep and sultry, and it surprises me a little. It's the first time I've sensed any dominance in him. A shiver runs down my spine, but I'm not afraid.

In fact, just the opposite.

How is this turning me on?

I feel a rush of heat in my body as Kit plants his hands on my desk. He leans forward, his eyes a bright gold, his body oozing angry male energy.

I meet his stare head-on while I clench my thighs under the desk.

"There are a lot of things that my father taught you that won't apply in the future. Don't think because you're his favorite you have any leverage with *me,*" Kit says, in a deep voice that makes my skin grow goose bumps.

I'm breathing a little unsteadily. He starts calming

down as we continue our face-off. His anger is replaced by something else, just as fierce and quiet.

"I suppose we got off to a bad start." I'm trying to appease him.

"Keep pushing me, and you'll get to see *bad*," he warns me. So he's not easily appeased.

Before I can answer, Kit storms out of the office and slams the door. Alone, I fully register the blazing warmth between my legs, the tingles on the back of my neck, my nipples pushing brazenly against my shirt.

What the hell has that man done to me?

I'm really worried about my argument with Kit hours later, and yet when I call to give my first report to Alastair and apologize for our altercation, he sounds thrilled.

"Congratulations, Alex, you've brought out my son's managerial qualities."

I sigh. "I didn't mean to. I feel really bad about it."

"Well *I* couldn't be more pleased. Report back soon," he says.

I sigh and rub my temples before I log off my computer and straighten my desk, then head home alone to make some pasta, text my sister and try to forget this day ever happened.

And later, as I get into bed and punch my pillow into shape, I can't help but wonder if I deliberately provoked my new boss. To get back at him for provoking me. In more ways than one.

Seven

I spend my entire weekend thinking about Kit. God knows why.

It's like he's etched into my mind.

It's even more irritating considering that I don't like him. Well, a part of me doesn't. About eighty percent of me. But the other twenty percent feels very differently. The guy ties my stomach in knots. Gives me butterflies. I can't decide how to describe it, but I don't like feelings that I can't control. This is definitely one of them.

I can't help but smart about having an argument with him, an argument where he was right. I made a fool of us both when I refused to call back the team. I know I humiliated him. Which is why I have to start this week out on a better foot or I'll risk losing my job.

It's Monday morning. A fresh week, a fresh start.

It's also judgment day for us all.

Today, Kit will head down to our department to take a look at the work we've done. Ultimately, it'll be his decision which design goes through. I hate having him decide. I don't need him to tell me whether I'm good at my job or not—I already know I am. Still, it requires his approval, so today, I'm on my best behavior. I so need this to go well, that I might even apologize to him.

I'm not my usual sharp self, and it doesn't help that the line at the coffee shop is so long that I have to skip it. I never consider myself fully awake without caffeine in my system, but for today, I'll have to make do.

When I arrive in the office, my team is already hard at work. I put my bag down on my desk chair. Tim looks up and smiles in greeting.

"Morning, Alexandra."

"Morning, Tim," I say. "It's good to see you all in early and in top form. Glad you're back with a better attitude, and I intend to have one, too."

"Nice speech, boss."

I turn and see Ellie walking in. She's grinning like nothing ever happened as she heads to her seat.

"All right, everyone. The boss will be coming in later to look over the final three designs. Let's blow him out of the water, shall we?"

Tim cheers and the rest of the team laughs. I roll my eyes, but I'm kind of glad I've gotten my office clown back. Today isn't going to be easy. But my team's excitement reminds me that even on difficult days, there can still be a reason to smile.

* * *

It's midafternoon and we've reviewed our designs endlessly by the time I have the courage to call Kit. I'm sitting in my mini-office at the back of the department, trying to muster the energy to go to battle with him. He's already scheduled to come and see the work we've done, but either he's forgotten or he's deliberately missed the appointment. I get the feeling it's the latter. He probably wants me to call him and beg for his attention. Pathetic.

I dial the phone number for the CEO suite—the number that used to belong to Alastair—and it rings several times.

"Yeah?" Kit finally answers.

I frown. "Is that how you greet your father's favorite and soon-to-be your favorite as well?" I tease.

"It's how I plan to answer when you show up on the caller ID, Ms. Croft. How can I help?"

I stiffen, taking the hit in stride and quickly say, "You were meant to come and see our designs and make a decision on the final look for the app."

"Was I? Oh, so your team is back to work? Are we certain we don't want them to take a few more days, just to be sure they're ready and recharged?"

I bite the inside of my cheek. I know he's trying to wind me up, so I keep a calm front. I don't want him having any sense of power over me. "We're ready, sir. Whenever you're ready, we've prepared a presentation."

"Well that should be just *riveting*," Kit says, his voice dripping with sarcasm. "I'll be down in two minutes."

He hangs up the phone without saying goodbye. I

know for a fact he won't be here in two minutes. He's going to make me wait as part of his game. I smile to myself, heading back into the main office to speak to my team.

"Mr. Walker will be with us shortly," I tell them. "Let's be ready to do the presentation in twenty minutes."

As suspected, Kit shows up late. When he looks to my face for a reaction, all he receives is a well-mannered smile. *Take that.* I know it's childish, but I'm so determined to dazzle him today. I don't know why.

Maybe it's guilt over our fight Friday. Maybe I'm just trying to get in my new boss's good graces. I don't like when I lose control, and he's caught me off guard several times already. Now, I'm determined to play it cool.

It would be nice if my heart got the message; it gives a little kick as Kit walks through the room.

He opts to ignore me, clearly aware his stunt didn't aggravate me. He rubs his hands together. "Right. Let's get on with it, shall we? What do you have for me?"

My skin prickles at his voice and I curse his gorgeous British accent to hell. Even Ellie, across the room, is eyeing him like he's the chef's special of the month.

As I show him the designs on the display screen, Tim tentatively pushes a portfolio toward Kit with a printout of the designs we will be showing him. "We've narrowed it down to three designs, sir."

Ignoring the screen on the wall, Kit takes the portfolio.

I smile. My design is at the back of the folder. Save the best until last, I say. Kit flips open the folder casually, flicking through the pages. There's weeks' worth of market research, color palettes and font designs in there. But I guess to someone like Kit, with no experience in the industry, all he sees is pretty colors on a page.

He lets out a long sigh as though everything in front of him displeases him. My heart freezes. What if he doesn't pick my design?

Kit throws the folder back on the table, clearly unbothered that he's tossing around people's hard work. "Who designed these?"

He lifts his gaze and looks at me.

I see the challenge there, but beneath that, I see intelligence. A lot of it.

"Ellie, Angela and I came out with the top designs," I tell him. "If you look up at the wall screen, the colors are more noticeable—"

I frantically work the remote, but Kit ignores the images zooming on the wall. He looks me in the eye and smirks.

"Well, I expect better from the 'best' design team in Chicago," Kit says, air quoting the word *best*. I blink.

"Excuse me?"

"You're excused. For now. But I expect better, Ms. Croft. From all of you," Kit says with a glint in his eye.

"There's nothing wrong with these designs."

"There's plenty wrong with the designs."

"Such as?"

"Well, where's the sex appeal? All these colors are stripped back and muted. If this is all you have, we might as well stick with the old design. At least it's erotic."

Angela giggles when he says this, which makes the entire situation even worse. I can't have my team swooning over this man when they're meant to be taking my side. I suck my teeth.

"If you read the brief your father sent, you would know that we're trying to move away from that type of design. A lot of our users are younger adults, and we need to make it more accessible to—"

"Right, that's all well and good, Ms. Croft, but I'm in charge now. I'm telling you, these designs are boring. They won't sell. I want you to start over."

Kit turns his back on us and starts to leave the room. He's showing his dominant side again. I almost gasp. I can't believe he's shot us down so savagely.

I stare at his broad back, his dark hair, every inch of me wanting to shake some sense into the guy or maybe do something else with him entirely. Something to appease the insane sexual tension crackling between us every time we bicker. Every time we're near. Every time those damn gorgeous, perceptive amber eyes lock on mine.

What is he doing to me?

Setting down the remote, I march after him, desperate to get him to see sense.

"You don't understand what you're saying. My team worked hard on this. You can't just discard everything we worked on."

Kit stops. He smiles. He moves back over to the table and picks up the folder, flicking through the papers again. He nods a few times and I wonder if by some miracle, he's actually changed his mind. He finds my design right at the back and takes it out, examining it in a better light. I feel my heart thudding against my ribcage.

Then I watch Kit set it back down.

Kit catches my eye.

A hot little shiver runs down my spine.

"Not. *Good*. Enough," he says. My design lies lonely on the table. Unwanted. His eyes are glistening with devilish glee. "My father expects me to bring it, Ms. Croft. And I… I expect you to bring it, as well. Now, try again."

Eight

It's been three days since Kit rejected the designs we worked so hard on. I haven't seen him since. The office has been quiet and somber. My whole team is crushed by the rejection. But I can't help feeling like I got the worst of it. The way he picked up my work and dropped it back down felt so personal. If we weren't at war before, we sure as hell are now.

Ellie has come over to my apartment tonight in an attempt to cheer me up, but I can't concentrate on the film she's chosen. It's not my thing at all, a thriller of some sort with an irritating male lead who is a constant reminder of why I can't seem to get along with most guys. I watch him tearing up his hometown with bullets and bombs, and I wonder to myself if all men are like that. Kit certainly is, leaving a trail of destruction in his wake. Honestly, I could spit fire right now. There's this horribly intense heat inside me, like I'm about to blow up at any moment.

I sink further into the sofa, wishing it would swallow me whole and end this constant state of fury that I've been feeling since Kit showed up.

"Come on, Alex, it's not that bad," Ellie says. I sigh, dipping my hand into the bowl of popcorn wedged between us.

"I'm in a terrible mood. I just can't believe I have to abandon weeks' worth of work for that idiot." I feel my hands clench into fists. Right now, I would love to hit the gym and punch the hell out of a boxing bag.

"Look, I know what happened, but you either need to do something about it or let it go."

"What would you suggest I do?"

"Report him to Alastair. No boss should get away with treating employees like that."

I sigh again, shifting my feet underneath me. "Yeah, well, I'm not exactly employee of the year. Sometimes I'm not a good boss, either."

"You are, I swear."

"Don't lie to me, Ellie. I pressure the team and nobody likes that. Now that Kit is pressuring me, I know how it feels to be on the receiving end of it." I stuff more popcorn in my mouth.

Ellie nudges me. "Stop feeling sorry for yourself. This isn't like you. Plus, have you noticed Ben eyeing you? I think he has a candle lit with your name on it."

"What?" It takes me a moment to realize who she's talking about. "Ben? I would never… Ben and I are friends. Just friends." I shake my head, finding the idea ridiculous.

"I'm worried about you," Ellie says. "You haven't been yourself since Kit arrived."

"Don't be worried. Just leave him to me."

Ellie shifts to face me. "Look, Alex, you're the best. The best at Cupid's Arrow. Hell, you're the best anywhere. Kit doesn't know what he's talking about."

I snort, but it's nice to hear someone say it. At least it boosts my confidence a little. "Thanks."

"He might not believe in you, but I swear, I do. I don't care if he's the boss. His opinion is zilch."

"You're the best, Ellie, really. Thank you for the pep talk." I smile at her and we both dig into the popcorn. "What do you think Angela and the other girls see in him?"

"Who?"

"Kit, obviously," I say. "They've been all over him like a rash since he arrived."

She rolls her eyes. "Like we don't know? He's got this certain something—this X factor. He's delicious. But of course, Angela is all over any guy like that. It's just the way she is."

"But everyone's talking about him. Even after what happened, I overhear them in the break room. They keep talking about all the girls he's hooked up with, or what color suit he's wearing. Angela seemed proud of herself when she discovered she drinks the same kind of coffee as him."

Ellie laughs, and I laugh, too. It's so stupid that it's comical. "Wow. What a dumb thing to get excited over," she says.

"Well, exactly, that's what I thought. That's why I just don't get it. He's an asshole. Women don't actually like that, right? I mean, there's really nothing to swoon over, is there?"

"Now who's trying to brainwash herself into thinking she doesn't like the new boss?"

I sigh. "You told me about those rumors from the night of Alastair's retirement party. I don't want anything to ruin Cupid's Arrow for me. I suppose that's why I've been so determined to almost hate Kit. A part of me wishes it was still Alastair in his place. Safe, nice Alastair."

"Alastair wants the good life. He's worked so many years, he deserves it. He won't come back, Alex."

"I know." I shoot her a wry smile, turning back to the TV. "I suppose all I can do is make the best out of my situation and try to get along with Kit. Yes, so he's got the women in a frenzy, but from now on, if being irresistible is his superpower, I'm completely immune to it."

Nine

I don't know how many new starts it's going to take to get things on track with Kit, but here I am, standing outside his office, ready to try again. I thought about what went down for a long time last night. I decided that my love for my sister and helping her through college, as well as my love for my job and this company, outweighs any hate or odd chemical reaction I have for him. That's why I have to stay and make amends, even if it means caving to a man I can't stand.

I take a deep breath and knock on Kit's office door. I hear a feminine giggle from inside and I immediately know he's got company.

"Can this wait?" Kit calls. I swallow back my anger, practicing my best civil smile from the safer side of his door.

"No, it can't," I reply through gritted teeth. There's silence inside for a moment. I clasp my hands together, pursing my lips.

I envision all sorts of things going on in there. Especially because it's Kit. It seems he can make anything feel naughty.

A moment later, the door swings open; Kit isn't smiling. He leans his arm against the door to prop it open and fixes me with an intense stare. I stare back, hoping he doesn't notice how heavy my breathing has become.

Then he opens the door all the way and lets out a middle-aged woman in a business suit. I start blushing when I realize they probably weren't hooking up like I thought they were.

"Thank you for your time, again, Kit, and say hello to your dad for me," the woman says.

Kit smiles charmingly and nods, then moves to allow me past.

"Come in, Miss Croft."

I step into his office. I can smell his cologne, and it makes my lungs feel greedy for another breath. I can't help it. I move to sit down in the spare office chair and watch him.

"I'm surprised that you're…getting into the groove of things so well."

To my surprise, Kit doesn't get angry. He laughs, shaking his head as he makes his way back to his desk. He sits down and puts his feet up.

I guess that's as good a start to the conversation as I could have hoped for. But then I remember why I'm here and fix my face into a stern frown. I'm not here to be friends. I'm here for the sake of business.

"How can I help you, Alex?" Kit asks. I notice he looks a little worse for wear. His voice catches like he's been smoking, and his eyes are raw from lack of sleep. Apparently taking on a full-time job hasn't stopped him from partying.

"I don't want anything in particular. But I do hope to find a way to work out our differences," I say, trying not to sound too invested. In fact, I need this meeting to go smoothly. I know I'm on thin ice already. I can't afford to slip up. "I thought we could maybe do lunch, or dinner, on a day you might be free…"

Kit's lips curve in a wicked smile. "Assuming I'm free," he corrects.

"So? Make me a priority," I tell him cheekily. "I *am* one of the most important employees you have on your payroll. I think we would do well to sit down together and get to know one another."

"Why not do that here?" Kit asks, amused by my retort. There's a softer look in his eyes, like he's coming around to the idea of us being friends instead of enemies.

I shrug, keen on getting him out of the office so we can step out of our formal roles a bit. We may have started on uneasy ground, but I'm pretty sure that having a moment to relax and relate to each other as people, not only boss and employee, could help. "I merely hoped to maybe find a place outside of work so we can both feel less stressed and more open with each other. But just so you're not mistaken, my intentions are purely business related. We'll be working closely together, and since you rejected my ideas for the app, I'd like to hear your thoughts on some new designs."

"About that—"

"I'm over it," I interrupt, but I keep my eyes on the desk instead of his face. "I just want to talk in a less formal setting. Maybe outside of office hours. I think it will relieve some of the…tension."

Kit smiles slowly, an intelligent spark in his eyes. "Is that what you want?"

"I'm sure you mean nothing by that," I say, an edge to my tone to warn him off. "But yes. That is what I want."

"All right. Dinner it is."

"Where would you like to meet? Are you available tonight?" I ask, balancing my work diary on my knee. Kit laughs.

"Well, Ms. Croft. You might have asked earlier. Some people have plans on a Friday night, you know."

My heart sinks a little. "Oh. Well, I guess I can do any time."

Kit smiles, kicking his feet off the desk and standing up. He puts his hands in his pockets, ever the image of the loveable scruff. Minus the loveable part.

"Well, I guess I'm free Monday evening."

"No dates lined up for the start of the week? How unusual," I tease. I know I'm pushing the boundaries, but hey, I have to get my own back somehow. Fortunately, he doesn't seem fazed. He smiles, leaning against his desk.

"Monday's a work night," he tells me. "Friday's for parties. In fact, I'm hosting one at my place tonight."

"How interesting for you," I say, already jotting dinner in for Monday. Kit shifts, clearly trying to get my attention, but I make a point of doodling in the margins.

"You should come," he finally says.

"No thanks," I reply a little too quickly. It's not that I don't like parties. I do. I just don't know if I want to be at one Kit is hosting—looking all gorgeous and sexy, relaxed after a full week's work. Years working under Alastair have taught me that these British boys enjoy a good party but I'm not here for that: work is my number one priority.

"Come on…half your department is going."

That catches my attention. "They were already invited?"

Kit smirks. "Well, I didn't think it would be your scene."

I close my diary with a loud thud, standing up. I'm not angry, as such. I'm just disappointed that none of my team told me about this. Now I look like an idiot.

"You thought right," I tell Kit with a slick smile. "I'll pass."

"Wait!" Kit says as I turn my back on him. Is that desperation I detect in his voice?

"I should have extended an invite earlier. I'd like you to come."

"Oh really?" I say, turning back to him. "Because we're such good colleagues?"

I can't help but dread that he didn't invite me because he was preparing to fire me.

"Because we should make an effort to get along," Kit says coolly. "You got your dinner date. Indulge me by coming tonight. I'm sure your co-workers will want you there, too."

I doubt that they would care either way, but he does have a point. He's doing the dinner on my terms, on my territory. I won that battle. I guess I don't have much of a choice. He's my new boss, after all. And I really want us to get along.

I suck my teeth, pretending to be indecisive if only to see Kit squirm. I bet it's not often a woman turns him down.

And why does it give me such pleasure to be the first? But I cannot indulge in this petty feeling for long.

Eventually, I nod.

"All right. I'll see if I can fit it in my busy schedule," I say, trying to keep things light. Kit's mouth twists into a grin.

"Ah, yes, you have *such* a busy schedule this evening."

I blush, but try to keep my cool. "My commitment to Netflix is pretty important to me."

"So it seems."

His eyes are laughing at me, taunting me. Somehow, though, this doesn't feel like Kit trying to get one over on me. It feels like banter.

There's an unexpected ease between us that wasn't there before. Maybe it's because we're alone, here in his office.

We're standing in the place where he's got the control. But with this meeting over, I feel like the one who's taken the wheel.

I turn to leave again, but Kit steps closer and takes my arm. "Alex. Can you wait a moment?"

I turn back to him. He's standing closer than we've ever been before. My breath catches in surprise, but I don't allow it to faze me.

I lift my chin, keeping my expression blank. Kit isn't smiling now. In fact, his tiredness looks even more intense now, and I can almost detect sadness in his eyes. Even in his worse-for-wear state, he still looks deliciously good, and I hate myself for recognizing it.

"I just wanted to say… I'm sorry for how I treated you the other day. I know it must have hurt you…and I apologize for that," Kit says.

I blink in surprise. I wasn't expecting that.

"Did your father put you up to this?"

"No, I didn't tell him. This is all me." Kit rakes a hand through his hair. It's only then that I register he's still holding my arm with his other hand. He fishes in his pocket and when he removes a paper from it, I immediately realize what it is.

It's a freshly printed—if slightly crumpled—copy of my design for the main page. I pull out of his grip to read over the page. It's covered with notes, presumably Kit's. At a glance, they're thoughtful and constructive.

"See you tonight, Ms. Croft," he says softly, opening his office door for me. I leave feeling even more conflicted than when I went in, asking myself the question: Is the real Kit the one who destroys people's work in the blink of an eye, or the man I just met in his office?

Ten

"Remind me again why I'm being dragged shopping with you?"

"Because you're a good friend and I asked you to. Okay, *begged* you to. And I *never* beg."

Ellie and I have been scoping out the shops for over an hour. As much as I love having nice clothes, I despise shopping.

I hate spending hours walking around, checking price tags, fighting for space in changing rooms and dealing with lines at the cash register.

Usually, I get my shopping fix online. I can try things on in the comfort of my home and avoid all the worst parts of shopping.

But today I've been forced to venture out. Kit's party is tonight and I have to have something killer to wear.

This isn't just my boss's party. This is a chance to show my worth.

What is the best way into a player's brain? A cute dress that shows off all the right things.

Okay. So maybe I also want to look fabulous because of that little quiver I had when I left his office earlier, but I don't plan to follow up on that quiver. My ego simply demands that I try to make him feel something, too.

I grab a silver dress from the rack, holding it up against me. "What do you think of this one?"

"Hmm…let me think…" Ellie pretends to be seriously deliberating, tapping the corner of her mouth. She rolls her eyes and drops her hand. "I think you'll look hot in it. Just like every single other dress you picked up."

I toss the dress over my outstretched arm with my other choices. "I have to look spectacular."

"For a work party?"

"This is different."

"Why? Because your boss isn't some old guy anymore? Are you trying to impress him?"

"Yes," I say honestly, flicking through the sales rack. "He's not like his dad. His dad had a little more class."

"So you're just going to go against everything you believe in? You're going to get drunk, wear a short dress just to impress a guy you don't even like, and then what? Are you looking for a raise or…? Admit it. You want him on his back…or you want to be on your back, on his desk…"

"Don't be ridiculous!" I snap, trying not to let myself get wound up by her words. She just doesn't understand. I'm not trying to get Kit's attention romantically. I'm trying to show I can be a part of his world. Then I'll make him a part of mine.

Work. I'm talking about work.

"Look, I impressed Alastair in other ways," I tell Ellie, collecting a few more dresses. My arm is starting to feel pretty weighed down. "I'm not after Kit. I'm just trying to appeal to his specific personality."

"Which is what?" Ellie teases.

"An idiotic player?" We both whirl around to spot Ben behind us, a smile on his face.

"Ben? What are you doing here?" I'm surprised as he greets us both with a nod, his eyes fixing on me. "So… you're falling for him just like every other woman in the office? I thought you were different, Alex." Ben smiles as if he's teasing me, but I'm confused by his words.

"Hey, I thought you liked Kit?" Ellie asks him.

"What gave you that impression?" Ben scoffs, dragging his feet as he follows us as we start around the store again.

"You were letting him lead you around like a puppy at the last party."

"Maybe that's how I impress the boss," he says, clearly taking a jab at me. "See, we don't all have to buy slinky dresses to do that."

I look Ben up and down, wondering what's up with him to be acting like such an ass. "Well, sure. I don't feel like Kit would be impressed if you showed up in a dress, now would he?"

Ben starts to argue back, but I laugh. "I'm teasing, Ben. Relax." I smile at him, and he seems to calm down.

I turn to the store assistant, showing her the number of items on my hangers. He smiles, nodding.

"All right. There's space for your boyfriend and friend to sit outside the changing rooms, if you'd like?"

I look back at Ben, realizing the store assistant is referring to him. "Oh, we're not…"

"Apologies." The store assistant smiles. "My mistake. Go on through."

Ben is blushing. I dump my outfits on a chair in the changing rooms, shutting the curtain.

"Look," Ben says, his voice slightly muffled by the curtain, "I just want to know if you've fallen for his charm like all the rest."

"Why would you think that?" Ellie demands.

"Well, she's trying hard to impress him at some dumb party. He didn't even invite her. She was an afterthought."

That hurts. Why is Ben being such a jerk? And how does he know I wasn't invited at first? I toss my work dress on the floor, trying not to take the bait.

"Look, this guy is my boss. Unless I quit and find another job, I have to try and be civil to him. You understand that, right? I'm not your boss but you have a team that sucks up to you, too."

"That's different."

"How is that any different at all?"

"Well, we're friends. We all get along at Cupid's Arrow."

"And if tonight goes well, Kit and I will be friends, too," I say, pulling on one of the dresses. "Or something that resembles friends, anyway."

"I don't get you at all," Ben grumbles.

"There's nothing to get. I'm just doing my job."

"Something changed. What was it?"

I don't want to tell him about my meeting with Kit today. I toss aside the first dress, unimpressed by how it looks, and grab the next one, How should I respond to Ben? How can I tell him that I sensed a shift in Kit? Not a massive one, but enough of a change that I no longer hate his guts. And also, why is he interrogating me?

"Alex? Are you ignoring me?"

"Can you please just drop it?" Ellie says.

I answer Ben then, just for friendship's sake. "I'm not interested in him in any way, shape or form. He's just my boss. I have to appeal to his better nature, if he actually has one. What's so hard to understand?"

"All right, all right. No need to get touchy. Both of you," Ben gripes.

I roll my eyes. How infuriating. Ben's the one who interrupted our shopping expedition and started this. I pull another dress over my head, expecting it to be too garish. But when I catch sight of myself in the mirror, I'm almost certain it's the one.

It's the silver dress, shiny like my glossy red hair. It's short, but not too short. Perfect to wear with heels.

I spin around and the dress glistens in the mirror's reflection. It dips a little at the front, showing just enough to catch the eye, but not so much that men will be staring at my breasts all night. I decide to test it out on Ellie and Ben. I open the curtain and peep my head around.

"What do you guys think?" I ask sweetly. Ellie gasps and immediately nods her head yes. Ben looks up from his phone and his jaw drops. I laugh at his expression.

"I'll get this one then. Shopping trip over. Thanks for the opinions, both of you."

When I step out, Ben composes himself a little. "Finally…"

"I'll see you at the party?" I ask.

Ben stands up, nodding. "See you."

After I pay for the dress and a matching clutch bag, Ellie and I head to the parking lot. "He definitely has his eye on you," Ellie declares.

"You're determined to hook me up with someone, aren't you? I like Ben. We're good friends. But that's all that there could ever be between us."

On the drive home, I remember how Ben looked at me in that tiny silver dress and smile.

I can't help but hope the dress has a similar effect on Kit.

Eleven

As I stand in front of my full-length mirror, I see everything that could go wrong tonight. With this dress, this party, this evening as a whole. Going to the party is the last thing I want to do.

The dress that I thought looked sexy and unique now looks tacky to me. What will Kit think if I show up looking like a glittery tart?

I examine myself closely. Is this what professional women wear to parties? Am I ridiculously overdressed—or the opposite? I've stared at myself so much now I can't even tell.

My mind keeps wandering back to Kit. Why do I care what he thinks? A million warning signs are flashing in my head. I'm getting too invested in this man.

He's my boss and nothing more. So why does it suddenly feel so important for him to like what he sees?

I have to get out of here before I change my mind.

Exhaling, I stroke my hair back from my face and search for the confidence I usually see in the mirror. For a moment, it's like looking at a stranger. A terrified stranger.

Breathe, Alex.

The last thing I want to do is back out, though, so I grab my keys and head downstairs. I drive to Kit's mansion in the Gold Coast, the only background noise the rumble of the engine and the radio, my nerves getting worse and worse.

When I spot his house in the distance, my stomach seizes up. I know that the minute I get out of the car I'll have a drink, despite all my rules.

I think I might need a few to get through this night.

I park in an enormous circular driveway among a million other cars.

It seems like I'm late, even though I'm right on time. I suddenly realize how popular Kit has become at Cupid's Arrow.

Is that why it's so important to me to get in his good graces? I don't know.

I kill the engine and lean back in my seat, exhaling when I spot Ben getting out of his car a few cars ahead of me. He seems relaxed as he spots me and comes over.

"Hey," I say, stepping out.

"You wore the dress."

I laugh. "Obviously. I got it for the occasion. Shall

we go in?" I ask him, trying to suppress my nerves as I motion to the door.

We head inside.

As I enter the huge foyer, I see a lot of familiar faces from work, but no Kit and no Ellie. She wanted to take her own car, and now I wonder if I should have insisted we come together.

A woman sweeps past with a tray of champagne and I snatch a glass, draining the liquid as fast as I can.

When I set the glass aside, I catch Tim and Angela looking at me from across the room, whispering to each other. I wipe my mouth. Let them talk. I have bigger problems. Though, to be honest, the champagne has gone straight to my head.

I meander through the grand house, picking up some drinks along the way, fuel for the evening ahead.

By the time I emerge by the outdoor pool, I have polished off my third glass of champagne.

That has to be a record for me.

Out here, there's drum and bass music playing. The pool is pink, lit by underwater lights, and several Cupid's Arrow staffers have stripped to their bathing suits to enjoy the water. Kit didn't tell me it was a pool party.

Feeling dizzy now, I search for Kit and see him lazing around on a lounger with a cocktail.

There are two women perched beside him, sopping wet from the pool. They hang on his every word in such a pitiful way, I snort. But they keep hovering around him, laughing at his jokes.

Something thick and slick worms through my veins. Jealousy.

I hate the feeling. And I hate that I've never felt jealous over a man before.

"Fine. So apparently, he can be funny," I mutter to myself, wobbling my way over to Kit. I turn a few heads along the way, but I can't figure out if it's my outfit or the sight of me letting lose that has caught people's attention.

Hopefully, it's the former, but I'm betting on the latter.

Kit spots me approaching and smiles slowly, biting his lip. The women are still jabbering away at him, but he's not listening anymore. I hold my head high, unsmiling.

At least the dress worked.

I finally have his full attention. He waves a dismissive hand at the two women and stands up as I come to a halt beside his lounger.

"If you'll excuse Miss Croft and me. We've got some business to discuss," he says, not even looking their way as he speaks to them. They get up reluctantly, but I'm too busy having a staring contest with Kit to care where they go next.

He sizes me up, his eyes hungry as he inspects me from head to toe. I'm a little unsteady on my feet, the slinky silver dress suddenly feeling one size smaller than the one I purchased at the store.

He swings his legs off the lounger and stands up to greet me with a handshake. "Good evening, Miss Croft. You look stunning."

My stomach clutches.

He's never told me that.

It's the sincere look in his eyes that gets me most of all.

"How are you?" he asks.

"I've been better," I admit, unable to completely shake the jealousy from my thoughts. I hiccup, covering my mouth in surprise. Kit grins.

"Had a few glasses of bubbly, have we?"

"One or two… I could use another."

"Are you sure about that? You're not exactly a party animal."

"Tonight, I'm anything I want to be," I declare. I'm not sure if it's my imagination, but my voice seems a little slurred.

Kit cocks his head at me. "You sure? You're already looking a bit…hazy."

"I'm a grown adult, Kit. If I want to have a drink, I will," I retort, though I'm suddenly aware that I don't sound like an adult. I sound like a little toddler who hasn't gotten her way.

I shake my head, reaching out to the ice bucket nearest the pool and pouring myself a glass of champagne. Kit smiles as he watches me, and I can't shake the feeling that this new me might actually have impressed him. I hold my glass up to him innocently.

"Cheers."

Kit raises an eyebrow. His smile is cunning.

"Cheers, indeed."

Ben appears at my side. He greets Kit, then turns to me.

"Hey, stranger." He smiles and draws me aside. He seems drunk. The girls from before pull Kit aside for a moment, too. I frown at Ben, mad that he interrupted me and Kit because…

I don't know why. Maybe it's that I'd barely pried him away from the other girls!

"You having a good time, Alex?" Ben asks me. He leans in a little and I can smell rum on his breath. And mint. It's almost as though he prepared for this moment. And all of a sudden, with a sinking heart, I know what's going on.

"I need… Kit. I need to talk to him." I try to turn away, a little dizzy from so much alcohol.

"He can wait, can't he?" Ben says with a coy smile, turning me back to him.

It's the kind of smile that might drive some women insane, but all it's doing for me is telling me that things are about to fall apart. Ben's lips dip toward mine and before I can change my mind, I turn my head. He collides with my cheek and I gasp, in both surprise and embarrassment.

Ben pulls away. Our eyes meet. His cheeks burn.

How did this happen?

I grasp at words, but Ben opts for silence. His lips are set in an unforgiving line.

"As I thought. A damn tease," he finally whispers.

Ben disappears inside before I can confront him about his outrageous behavior. I touch my lips, wondering what would have happened if I hadn't turned my head in time. What the hell was he thinking? Did I ever give him the impression that I wanted that? No, we work together, and more importantly, I'm his friend.

Even worse?

Kit was watching.

My heart sinks as I become aware of the stillness around me.

I lift my head and meet his amber gaze. He has an expression I've never seen before. The women are talking to him, but it's as if nobody else exists but me.

He takes a step, his expression tight and fierce with passion and possessiveness. "You all right, Alex?" he asks. His voice is deathly quiet. His breath warm atop my head as he reaches me. He smells of alcohol and coffee, of his cologne; he smells like the guy I want. I tip my face up, dizzied by his presence.

"I'm fine." I reach out and grab his glass and drain it for him. "Never been better. Boss." I grin up at him. His eyes are gleaming. He glances at Ben's retreating figure and it makes my heart skip.

"Don't do that," I whisper.

He looks down at me. "Do what?" His voice is huskier than normal, too.

"Look all sexy and possessive over me. I'm having enough trouble keeping my mind straight around you without you complicating things."

The surprise on his face is priceless. "Is that a fact?" he purrs, his eyes twinkling wickedly.

"Fact!" I nod my head up and down. I stumble a little, and reach out to grab his arm to steady myself. "Ooops." I smile at him, aware of his firm muscles. "Wow, you're fit."

He reaches up to hold me by the elbow, keeping me steady.

"Why don't we sit you down, Ms. Croft?" His eyes

are twinkling, and I nod as he leads me to the lounger. I care about nothing else but the way he's looking at me right now.

I catch a glimpse of Kit's watch. It's midnight.

Why am I holding my boss's wrist in my hand? I can't tell you. The past few hours have been a blur. It takes me a moment to realize that I'm talking, my brain working several seconds slower than my tongue.

"I work my ass off, you know," I say, looking up with blurry eyes to see Kit's features swimming in front of me.

"Of course you do."

"And then you walk in and you just trample all over me," I blurt. My words seem to be coming out faster than I can handle. How did this conversation begin?

"Is it possible you're taking this too personally, Miss Croft?"

"Oh, I insure you, it is personal," I hiss, before realizing I used the wrong word. I shake my head in frustration. "Assure, damn it, not *insure*."

"I'm sure everyone understood what you meant."

Everyone? I look up. A small crowd has gathered to hear my ranting. I press the edge of my hand to my forehead. This isn't going well.

"Come here, Alex, let's talk about this in private." Kit doesn't sound angry. He ushers me to my feet, holding my elbow as he leads me to a shadowed alcove behind the pool cabana. He looks over at the people we left behind.

"I think we should definitely talk about this and I

think *you* should listen for once," I continue. "You're not used to that, are you? Not used to being challenged? Well here I am, Kit. I'll show you a challenge."

I wait for him to get angry now, but Kit seems more amused than anything. I notice my hand is still clasped on his wrist while his other hand remains on my elbow, keeping me on my feet.

"Have you got a lift home?" Kit asks me, studying my features.

"Home?" I'm heartbroken that he wants to send me home when I can feel the warmth of his touch. Suddenly I've never felt this content. "I'm not going until we've resolved this, Mr. Walker." I speak to him as if he were a child.

"I think I see your friend…hey, Ellie, is it?"

Through my blurred vision, I spot Ellie approaching. "Hey. Alex. *Alex?*"

She gapes at me, and I blink.

"Wow. Is it bad?" she asks Kit.

"Your friend is a little…well, intoxicated. Are you taking her home?"

I peer at Kit and notice his expression is closed off. As if he's guarding a secret. I bristle that he's so eager to get rid of me.

"I'm not going home. I brought my car here and I'm not leaving without it," I argue, glaring at him. Wondering why he can be so handsome and so hardheaded at times. I thought we were having a good time here!

"We can come get your car tomorrow. Come on, Alex," Ellie tells me, reaching out.

I swat the air to keep her hand away and grip Kit's

wrist tighter and shake my head. "Not yet, Ells! I'm having a *good* conversation with our new boss and he's at last *listening*," I say in glee. "I have yet to tell him how he should never dismiss his employees' hard work so blatantly to their faces…"

"Alex." Ellie puts her face in her hands, then laughs. "God, I'm sorry, Kit. She never drinks. So when she does…"

"Right," I hear my boss say, his beautiful British accent close to my ear.

"God, even your accent is sexy," I mumble, shaking my head.

Ellie's eyes flare. "Alexandra," she whispers.

I blink.

I hear a husky chuckle of disbelief from Kit.

Kit leans closer to my ear. "You hate me one second and the next you like my voice. Ah, Ms. Croft, we really need to get our heads on straight, don't we?" He looks at me, eyes twinkling, as he shakes his head.

"Ellie, give me half an hour more," I plead. I don't want to go. I want to kiss him. I want him to keep teasing me. Looking at me like that. Suddenly I've never wanted anything as much as I want him right now.

Ellie looks worried.

"I'll drive her home," Kit tells her.

An awkward silence hangs in the air. There's a warm protectiveness in his expression as he regards me. Suddenly I feel clearer now than I have in hours. Part of me knows this moment is significant. This is the make or break of our relationship. My boss just offered to drive little insignificant me home.

I suppose it's a start. A good start.

"Thank you, Kit, I like being with you. It's very refreshing and invigorating to chat with you," I tell him. "Ben tried to kiss me," I whisper, a confession.

"I know." Kit narrows his eyes.

"I'm just telling you because I don't want you to think that, if you tried, that I'd…give you the cheek as well."

"Alex," Ellie says more urgently now. She steps forward and whispers to Kit. He agrees to whatever she says and hands my elbow over to Ellie. Everything is muffled all of a sudden. I try to walk back to Kit, to go where I'm safe, but the whole world is suddenly spinning.

I trip and feel myself fall, but I don't seem to land. Strong, hard arms catch me even as I just keep falling, the world dissolving into nothing around me.

Twelve

I wake up with a pounding headache and no clue where I am.

I sit up, trying not to let the dizziness send me sprawling back onto the bed. When I look around me, I notice that I'm in a huge bedroom that certainly isn't mine. I take in the sparse masculine decor and quickly deduce this must still be Kit's house. I groan, falling back onto my pillow. This morning is a brutal reminder of why I don't drink.

I try to sort out my thoughts as I lie in the dark, regretting everything I can't remember. Fragments of the night come back to me, the shards of memory slicing through my headache like a knife. I remember Ben trying to kiss me. I remember sauntering up to Kit in my sparkly dress. When I look down, I see that I'm still wearing it.

Worst of all, the memory of shouting at Kit comes back. Me, responsible workaholic, shouting at Kit, my boss, about "challenges." All those people watching me make an idiot of myself.

God! Why did I do it?

And then later…

Oh my God!

Was I coming on to my boss?

I was supposed to be getting in his good graces. Now, all I've managed to do is guarantee that I'm getting fired. *Way to go, Alex.*

I'm an absolute imbecile. I can't believe he even let me stay in his house after the way I behaved.

And did he…did he catch me when I passed out?

Heat suffuses my cheeks as I remember his arms around me. Every pore in my body is certain that it was Kit who caught me when Ellie tried to take me home. Kit who maybe…*carried me into his bedroom?*

I feel another wave of humiliation and embarrassment.

I lie in the dark for some time before I hear the knock on the door.

Kit pokes his head in. He's stoic and unsmiling but he doesn't look too angry.

"Feeling tender this morning, Miss Croft?" he asks smugly as I peek at him from my duvet cave.

I close my eyes. "I'm so sorry."

"It happens to the best of us, Alex. Sit up. I've brought you a drink." He shuts the door behind him and crosses the room.

He looks good enough to eat. Devour. But I really,

really *shouldn't* have such thoughts, even though he's the only thing I seem to have an appetite for.

"I really couldn't stomach coffee right now…"

"It's not coffee. It's something better," Kit assures me.

I feel so humiliated I just want to hide under the covers and never come out, but I know I have to indulge him. I'm walking a very thin line between having a job and being spectacularly fired.

I prop up the pillows behind me and lean back. Fortunately, Kit doesn't turn the light on, which is good for two reasons: one, because my eyes are extremely sensitive right now, and two, I don't want him to see how much of a mess I am.

Another wave of embarrassment pulses through me. If there was one person I wanted to impress last night, it was my boss. Now look what I did.

He hands me a glass of something clear and fizzy. I wrinkle my nose.

"Did you just hand me a vodka and lemonade?"

Kit laughs softly. The noise hurts my head, but it's actually quite nice to hear him laughing so freely after what happened last night.

"No, I'm not a sadist, Alex."

"My mistake," I say before I can stop myself. "I just thought…"

"Trust me, it's lemonade with added sugar. My mum used to make it for me when I was feeling poorly. It works a treat for hangovers."

"Oh." Leaning forward, I sip the bittersweet drink, trying to remember if my mom did anything like that.

After I left for college, I mostly stayed in contact with my sister, Helena. So no.

It tastes pretty good. For a moment, I think my headache even improves. I glance at him, wondering about his relationship with his mother. "So your mum…" I say with an exaggerated British accent, smiling. "Do you see her often?"

"She's back in London. So…no. But we talk. I make sure she's well." He looks at me curiously, then tilts his head at an angle and narrows his eyes. "You?" The huskiness of his voice reminds me of the intimacy of being so close to him last night. I glance at my elbow, remembering his touch. Wanting it again.

Get a grip, Alex.

I shake my head, praying he doesn't see the pink I feel coming into my cheeks. "My parents…well, my sister and I basically raised ourselves. They're workaholics. I suppose you have them to thank for my work ethic, and why I'm so devoted to Cupid's Arrow. It's one good thing I learned from them."

"So all your other strengths I should attribute to you alone?"

I suddenly blush head to toe to hear him say this. I'm secretly frustrated at myself for letting this guy get to me so easily.

Kit looks smug, standing by the edge of the bed. "Well, what a night…"

I scowl, irked that he gets to look so handsome this morning when I'm in such sad shape. "Look, if you've come to revel in my misery, I'll leave right now."

"Oh come on, Alex. You have to admit it was funny."

"Funny? You think me being a drunken mess and abusing my boss is funny?"

"Well if I can see the funny side, I think you should be able to as well."

"You're maddening!"

"And you think you're not? I could've fired you on the spot, Alex. But I'm willing to look past it because I know these things happen. And I know you didn't mean it."

"Well, I did…"

Kit chuckles, shaking his head. "Not everything," he says softly, his gaze a little more intimate. "And you really aren't helping your cause. All right, you meant it. At least the bad part of it. Every word of it. At least you were honest."

"Really?"

Kit shrugs. "Sure. It makes sense, and I forgive you for that. I can be a bit of an ass, I admit." He pauses and smiles, almost to himself. "You thought my accent sexy."

"I didn't say that!"

"Oh come on, Alex. I thought you had a sense of humor…"

"I do, when something is funny."

"Looks like I'm not the one with the problem. May I remind you that I just came in here with a peace offering?" He shoots me a hard look.

"You mean *lemonade*? That's your *peace offering*?"

"I thought you coming to my party meant you had lightened up a bit. But no. You spent the entire night laughing and joking with me, only to turn at the last moment. You said I was arrogant, rude, bossy, unreasonable…just about every insult under the bloody sun. Take a hard look in the mirror, Alex. I think you will find that you are all those things and more. But here I am, willing to give you the benefit of the doubt."

I'm a little shocked. I never expected him to be so affected by something I said when I was drunk. But there's a fierce vulnerability in his eyes, even though he's angry. I realize that whatever I said last night must have really gotten to him. And he's right. I *am* all of those things. He's right in saying that I'm being hypocritical. I shrink back into myself. I need to cool it.

"Look, I'm sorry," I tell him, and I mean it.

He shrugs. "It's nothing. I just thought we should hash things out."

"Yeah. Sure, of course."

Kit smiles and the flirtatious twinkle returns to his eyes. Any trace of sadness is gone so quickly, I'm not entirely sure it was ever there.

"You'll grow to like me. I know it." He sits at the foot of the bed and puts a hand on my feet, which poke up under the duvet. He grasps them through the fabric in a friendly, almost brotherly way.

I wiggle my toes against his palm and try for a half smile. "I wouldn't push your luck."

I glance down and admire his big tanned hand. He's cupping my arches. The warmth of his touch even through the duvet, makes me forget my pounding headache.

Suddenly I remember him stopping my fall last night with such clarity, I'm flustered. "Thanks for catching me last night," I whisper, my voice changing as I raise my eyes to his.

"I'll always catch you, Alex." He speaks naturally as if there is no doubt in his mind that he would. His eyes look a little darker and unreadable. Suddenly he glances down at his hand, as if he didn't realize his thumb was caressing my feet through the fabric until now.

Kit lets go of my feet and stands up. "That's what I do best, Alex. Push my luck, I mean. Are you fit to drive yourself home, or shall I call you a taxi?"

"A taxi might be best." I'm not feeling up to driving at all.

"I assume dinner is still on for Monday?"

My cheeks are blazing hot, and my nipples are poking into my bra so hard that they hurt. I'm just glad I'm mostly hidden under the duvet.

God. The last thing I want to do is spend more time with Kit, especially with how crazy he makes me. However, I'm not giving up an opportunity to level with him. I have to go through with it.

"I'll be there."

"I'm free tonight. If you are."

I meet his gaze, my breath catching.

I should keep it on Monday. We both should. But I whisper, "I'm free, too."

His eyes flash unexpectedly, and a brief smile curves the corner of his lips. "Good. See you tonight then," Kit says as he leaves the room. I watch him disappear and hear him talking on the phone in the corridor.

Strangely, the second he leaves, I wish he would come back and spend more time with me.

Thirteen

I take the taxi home in shame. Somehow, I feel worse after speaking to Kit. Maybe because he was so sympathetic and I don't understand what's going on between us. He certainly didn't have to be so nice to me today, after the way I acted. I press my throbbing head against the cold glass of the taxi window, still feeling the effects of last night as Chicago whizzes past me.

When the car pulls up outside my apartment, I pay the driver myself, despite Kit insisting he would cover the bill. I don't want to owe him anything else. I already owe him for giving me a second chance. I sigh as I step out of the car.

This business with Kit is tiring me out.

He's been in my life for only a few weeks and he has completely and utterly undone me. At least tonight will be on my terms. It will be my chance to talk to him about the designs. Smooth things over between us. This dinner kind of puts the ball back in my court. The trouble is, I don't seem to know how to handle the ball when Kit hits it to me.

Inside my apartment, I quickly change our reservation to tonight. I text the details to Kit. It's at my favorite Italian restaurant, Luciano's, a small quiet place I've been to with Kit's father. He approved, so hopefully, his son will be just as keen. With so much resting on this night, I know it has to go perfectly.

I take a long hot shower and then put on some sweatpants—a rarity for me—to slob around in front of the TV. There's some rerun of an old sitcom on but I'm not really concentrating. My mind is plagued by memories of the party. Every few minutes, I find myself cringing as I recall something dumb I said or did.

My hangover subsides by four o'clock and I take to going online and checking my social media. I think of Ben and wonder what got into him. I'm angry that he stepped over the line, but considering we were all drunk and I did something I regret with Kit, too, I can't blame him. I'm willing to forgive that. But I still worry. What if this is the end of our friendship? Over some dumb kiss. Not even that, because it didn't actually happen. Is Ben so up his own butt that he can't handle being rejected?

Somehow, I think he is.

Sighing, I keep scrolling through my apps. I absent-mindedly like a few pictures posted by family, friends and co-workers. I stop when I find what I'm looking for.

Ben posted a photo less than an hour ago. It's a group shot of him and a bunch of other people. I recognize Tim and Angela's smiling faces, but the rest are strangers to me. There must be ten of them in the image, all out for a meal today downtown. It's hard not to feel the punch of being left out.

Ben deliberately didn't invite me, but did he intend for me to see this?

I stare at the photo for quite some time until Ben's smiling face becomes a blur. Then I read the caption over and over until the hurt of what it says sinks in.

Always remember who your real friends are!

It stings like a bee. My eyes cloud with tears, but I wipe them furiously. I know there is no point being upset over this idiot. I did nothing wrong. He's the one getting butthurt because he can't handle it when a woman says no.

I shake my head, throwing my phone down on the couch and heading to my bedroom to get ready. I think about Kit and how he cared for me this morning. No, Kit is not my friend. Yes, Kit can be an arrogant idiot. But at least he's not punishing me. He has every right to, unlike Ben. And yet he's the one taking the high road.

What does that say about men like Ben and men like Kit?

Well, I've had enough. Truly. I've made plenty of mistakes this weekend but rejecting Ben definitely wasn't one of them.

I catch sight of my mournful face in my mirror and stick my chin up defiantly. I don't need guys like him wasting my time. I have a dinner to prepare for.

* * *

I arrive early at Luciano's, but Kit is already waiting for me. He smiles when he sees me. When I smile back, for once it isn't forced.

I'm dressed more comfortably this evening in a little black dress and my favorite red shoes. I notice Kit has made an effort, too. His shirt is ironed and only his top button is left undone. His suit is stylish and sharp. He looks like the businessman his father wants him to be. Together, we are picture perfect. Pure class and ready to get down to business. No one would suspect that last night I was a drunken mess shouting at my boss. No one can tell there's tension between us. For tonight, we are a ready for anything.

"Evening, Alex," Kit murmurs, offering his arm to me. "Shall we?"

I take it with a curt nod and a smile that's all business, trying to quell the odd flutterings in the pit of my stomach.

"Let's do this."

As we are led to our table, I can feel Kit's eyes on my back. I feel like he must be checking me out, but I can't decide how that makes me feel.

Do I like it?

Maybe a little.

A little *too much*.

I shake my head to myself. This is ridiculous. I need to keep my focus. I'm not here to flirt or be flirted with. This is a business meeting.

The waiter leaves us with some menus and Kit pulls

out my chair for me. I nod to him graciously and his smile lingers as he too takes his seat.

"You're killing it in that dress, Alex," he says. For once, though, he doesn't seem smarmy or overly flirtatious. He's just being nice. My cheeks burn.

"You're too kind, but flattery will get you nowhere."

Kit smiles before hiding his face behind his menu. "Who says I'm trying to get somewhere?"

"Oh, I'm almost certain you always have a destination in mind."

Kit's face reappears from behind the menu for a moment. "Not tonight. Let's just have a good talk, yeah?"

I nod, focusing on the menu, my cheeks still burning. Now that we're on civil terms, I'm very aware that I'm out in public with a very handsome man.

The same man that has been driving me to insanity, able to make me blush with a simple compliment.

Of course this is why the women in the office fall so easily at his feet, and I hate that I can perfectly understand their point of view.

The waiter returns with a notepad. He clicks his pen several times, fixing us with his best smile.

"Wine?"

Kit's eyes meet mine. A simple eyebrow flick from him and a nod from me confirms that we will. I'm breaking my own rule already, but one glass won't hurt.

"Red, white or rosé?"

"Always red for me," Kit says.

To me, it tastes like vinegar, but I allow Kit to choose an expensive sounding wine that puts a smile on his face.

We pick our appetizers and entrées and the waiter

leaves. I rub my hands together, finally in my element. I already have half a speech prepared for the new designs I want to pitch.

"So, I've been thinking a lot about your criticisms of the app design. I really liked your thoughts on the markup you gave me. I had to make a lot of changes since the brief is now completely different but I think you'll be pleased this time."

Kit regards me in silence, easing his chair forward. "I'm glad." A smile curves his lips.

Lips I wanted to kiss me only last night. I shake the thought aside.

"We got off to a bad start," he continues. "You were right about me. I am arrogant. I did want to be in control. I did want to belittle you to strengthen my own position. And… I turned down your ideas out of spite— though I still knew you weren't giving me as good as I knew you could."

I blink twice, wondering if I'm imagining this entire scene. "What are you saying?"

"I'm saying…let's face it, you're the best in this business. But I knew you could give me more."

I blush. "Kit… I don't know what to say. Thank you. I'm glad you pushed me."

He looks up at me sheepishly, his thick eyelashes framing warm and sincere eyes. It's a new look on him, but it suits him. "I'm glad you came back from it even stronger. I can look at your latest changes to the design Monday and we can move on from this mess. Deal? We're almost to the point where I can give my final approval."

"Absolutely. Deal."

"Thank you, Alex. Honestly, I have more than the company's future riding on this. I'm determined to prove to my father I'm my own man. And if you're willing… I would love to work more closely with you. I guess I'm open now to having you as a mentor. What do you think?"

I'm shocked at his newfound attitude. He wants me to help him? I can't tell if he's for real or this is another windup. Or is he afraid I'll tattle on him to his dad? But when I study his face, he looks genuine.

He's watching me closely, waiting for a reaction. I hold his stare for a while, taking a deep breath.

"I think a boy like you needs a lot of training, but I can knock you into shape," I tease, smiling to let him know I'm joking. He grins, leaning back casually in his seat.

He finally looks his usual at-ease self.

"Excellent," he says. "So I guess it's time we got to know one another."

"I guess so." I regard him with curiosity. "What you just said about proving yourself to your father. Is there a particular reason he'd think you're not fit to run the company?"

"He believes I'm exactly like him. And he wanted me to be a copy of my older brother instead."

Kit says it so calmly, as if it doesn't matter, but I almost wince. I know that my parents always favored me over Helena, and it always broke my heart to see her so devastated by that. It's not fair to see me as better than my sister because I got a job before I even finished college. She'll get to the top, I know it. But not everyone is on the same timeline to success.

"Do you talk to your brother?"

"Sure. Why?" He frowns.

I shrug. "I don't know. I just wondered if there was any competition between you two because of what you said."

"Of course there is. We're both healthy males. He wants to be the best and so do I." Kit leans forward, the sparkle in his eyes devilish. "I admit, he's got a couple of years' head start in the business world, and he's more anal retentive than I ever want to be. But I'll be happy to prove to him and to my father both that I'm my own man."

"You sound determined." I'm smiling, but worried that I'm finding Kit more and more irresistible by the minute.

"Does that mean you believe I can be serious about something in my life, Alexandra?" He winks, and my stomach takes a little pleasurable dip.

I laugh and nod.

"It's time you told me about you now."

He mimes getting out a microphone, holding it to his mouth like an interviewer. "So I'm on the red carpet with Miss Alexandra Croft, who is here representing Cupid's Arrow and their first blockbuster romance movie. Miss Croft, what are your hopes and dreams?"

I shake my head with a dry chuckle. "Well, getting through a meal with my boss without wanting to kill him might be a good start."

"Why, Miss Croft? Is he a terrible boss or simply

too good to stand?" Kit says, keeping up the act. "And do you think you'll manage to work with him peacefully in the future?"

"Well, he's been reasonably charming lately, so I suppose it's possible," I say with a sly smile.

I'm surprised by how much I'm enjoying this little game. Kit leans forward, finished with his imaginary microphone.

"My, my, Alex. If I didn't know better, I would say that was a little flirtatious."

I lean forward, too.

Our faces are closer than they've ever been, and my heart is racing.

"Well, it's a good thing you know better, then."

Kit smiles, his imaginary microphone returning, his timbre dropping. "Miss Croft, you are what most men would describe as a 'tough nut to crack.' How does one go about capturing your heart? Are you a fan of the classic wine and dine tactic?"

"Well, I believe in getting to know each other's tastes gradually, not prying," I say pointedly, "however, I do have some things that I like on a date…"

"Such as?"

"Roses."

"Ahh, classic."

"But not red ones."

Kit leans back in his seat, his eyes never leaving mine. "Really?" The microphone is gone. The whole game is over. He seems genuinely interested in my answer.

"Black is more my type."

"I should have known. Why black?"

I smile. "Because they are as sinister as they are beautiful."

He watches me closely. "So you have a sinister side?"

"Not really. I think I look tougher than I am," I admit. Cheeks getting hot.

"Do you now?" His voice is soft, almost tender. "Somehow I should've known that."

I crack up, hoping that Kit puts my blushing down to my laughter. "Wow, I can't decide if that's a compliment or an insult."

Kit smiles a slow, devilish smile. "The best comments are both, in my experience. Black roses…well, you're full of surprises, Alexandra Croft." He tuts and shakes his head, eyes twinkling.

"Well you can't say that you don't find them interesting. I mean, they're gorgeous to look at in a unique sort of way. And the fact that they look a little brooding makes it even more pleasant when you get up close and smell their lively, irresistible aroma."

The waiter returns with the wine and pours us each a glass. Kit is still regarding me with a small chuckle at my words as I raise mine in a toast to my boss, finally at ease in his company.

"Here's to constantly surprising one another," Kit says, clinking his glass against mine.

It's late by the time we leave the restaurant. I've had two glasses of wine and everything is making me giggle, but I'm not sure if it's the alcohol or Kit that's making me so merry. He threads his arm through mine as we walk toward the taxi rank at a hotel only a block away, and I cling to him, trying not to topple on my high heels.

"I don't think alcohol is your strong point, Miss Croft."

"I agree entirely. I feel like newborn Bambi. Stumbling all over the place."

"Right. When we do this again, we'll stick to water."

I stop to stare at him. "When we...again?"

Kit suddenly seems nervous, his arm limp in mine, his jaw squaring as he flexes a muscle in the back. He lets go of my hand and rubs the back of his neck, glancing around before his gaze fastens to mine. His stare is dark and unreadable all of a sudden as he grasps my hand again, speaking slowly, as if every word is important. "Well, I thought as colleagues, we could do it again. We should. For the purpose of business. Don't you agree, Alex?" His stare is intent, his eyebrows furrowing as he waits for my answer.

"Business," I say quietly, testing the word on my tongue.

Somehow, tonight didn't feel like business. It felt like friendship. It felt like fun. It felt like...the start of something.

It felt...so *good* in a way I haven't experienced in a while.

A taxi pulls up and Kit's arm falls away from mine. He moves to open the door for me with a quiet smile that melts my heart. It's so much better than his playboy bullshit. This is the real Kit. I'm convinced of it.

"Until next time?" he asks, his voice simultaneously quiet and gruff, his accent almost thicker for some reason. He stares at my profile with such intensity I feel breathless.

I don't know why. Impulse. Need. Happiness. The wine. The evening. Or Kit. Just Kit. But I lean in and kiss his cheek gently, the warm fuzz of the wine making me smile against the stubble on his hard jaw.

"Until next time," I promise.

I ease back and meet his gaze, noticing the dark flecks inside his amber eyes, noticing the look of shock on his face as I, too, start to feel stunned by what I did.

Did I just kiss Kit?

Why did I do that?

Kit looks down at me with this gorgeous smile in his eyes, and I lick my lips, nervous about this new step I've taken with him. I start to turn around when he lifts his hand, and cups my cheek in his warm palm. Tipping my face up, he sweeps down to set a kiss on one of my cheeks as well. I gasp in surprise, my mouth parting as Kit nudges my nose with his, and leans down to set another kiss on my other cheek.

I'm completely breathless. Turned on. Aching. Trembling down to the toes of my feet. Maybe it's the alcohol, but I know that it's not. It's actually him…nuzzling me again as he raises his lips to set one last kiss on my forehead.

"Good night." He leans back, the hottest guy I've ever met, smiling down at me in a way that makes every cell in my body quiver.

Swallowing back the hot lump of desire in my throat, I turn around, desperate to get away from him, from myself, from the things he makes me feel. I get into the taxi and tell the driver my address. As the car pulls away, my eyes meet Kit's and we watch each other until he's just a spot in the distance.

My stomach is in chaos, and there's something in my veins that wasn't there before. That's never been there before. Kit smelled so good when I kissed him. I hope he didn't notice that I couldn't quite breathe.

That the one breath I took was just so I could breathe him in deeper.

Fourteen

How's Kit doing? The boy living up to his potential yet?
Still waiting for a report.

I blink in the shadows of my bedroom early Sunday
morning when I see the text from Alastair.

I don't know how to answer. Kit has been surprising me, at every turn. I'm also a little bit remorseful
over the fact that I spent all night having erotic dreams
about my new boss.

He's surpassing expectations. Determined to bring
only good things to Cupid's Arrow.

Impressed? I told you there was more to him than his
reputation...

Get Up To 4 Free Books!

Dear Reader,

IT'S A FACT: if you answer 4 quick questions, we'll send you 4 FREE REWARDS from each series you try!

Try **Harlequin® Desire** books featuring heroes who have it all: wealth, status, incredible good looks...everything but the right woman.

Try **Harlequin Presents® Larger-print** books featuring a sensational and sophisticated world of international romance where sinfully tempting heroes ignite passion.

Or **TRY BOTH!**

I'm not kidding you. As a leading publisher of women's fiction, we value your opinions... and your time. That's why we are prepared to reward you handsomely for completing our mini-survey. In fact, we have 4 Free Rewards for you, including 2 free books and 2 free gifts from each series you try!

Thank you for participating in our survey,

Pam Powers

To get your 4 FREE REWARDS:
Complete the survey below and return the insert today to receive up to 4 FREE BOOKS and FREE GIFTS guaranteed!

"4 for 4" MINI-SURVEY

1 Is reading one of your favorite hobbies?

☐ YES ☐ NO

2 Do you prefer to read instead of watch TV?

☐ YES ☐ NO

3 Do you read newspapers and magazines?

☐ YES ☐ NO

4 Do you enjoy trying new book series with FREE BOOKS?

☐ YES ☐ NO

Please send me my Free Rewards, consisting of **2 Free Books from each series I select** and **Free Mystery Gifts**. I understand that I am under no obligation to buy anything, as explained on the back of this card.

❏ **Harlequin® Desire** (225/326 HDL GNWK)
❏ **Harlequin Presents® Larger-print** (176/376 HDL GNWK)
❏ **Try Both** (225/326/176/376 HDL GNSV)

FIRST NAME	LAST NAME

ADDRESS

APT.#	CITY

STATE/PROV.	ZIP/POSTAL CODE

READER SERVICE—Here's how it works:

We'll see.

Report again soon.

I exhale nervously and put my phone back on my nightstand. I'm dreading every time I hear from Alastair, trying to avoid reporting on anything, and that makes me feel bad. I don't want to even think about why I'm avoiding this responsibility. He expects a full report. But I don't want to be ratting on Kit. Even if he makes a mistake… I would like to think, after tonight, that I can help him through any rough patches. I'm only in charge of one department of the company, but getting to know more of Kit, I'm beginning to admire him. His input on the app design was honest, and more than that, it was good. To the point. He wants his company to succeed as much as I do, or more. He has a thirst for proving himself to his father and I, suddenly, really hope that he does. So does that make me biased, unable to fulfill my mission for Alastair? And is last night's kiss clouding my judgment?

I sigh as I press my cheek back into my pillow and inhale the lingering scent of him in my nostrils, shutting my eyes and blaming Kit Walker for the fact that I can't go back to sleep.

I've picked up my car from Kit's place—finally. And on Monday, for the first time possibly ever, I'm torn about going in to the office. On one hand, I'm sort of dying to see Kit, even though I'm frustrated at myself for feeling like this. On the other, I'm not looking forward to dealing with the whole Ben thing.

Cupid's Arrow used to be a place where I felt safe, accepted, even admired, perhaps. But today, I'm heading there with the knowledge that it'll be awkward when I see Ben. Plus, there's the nerve-wracking knowledge that I'm a little bit too attracted to my boss and I don't know what's happening between us.

When I step through the doors of the main office, Tim and Angela start clapping. I groan, remembering the fiasco at Kit's place. Tim even throws in a cheesy wave for good measure.

I try not to roll my eyes at them.

If they're going to celebrate the fact that I made a fool of myself at Kit's party, then I can't really say I didn't have it coming. Still, I can't help but blush at their antics.

"Way to go, Alex! The girl can let loose!" Tim cries.

"Okay, enough," I stop them, chuckling before I force myself to get serious.

Last weekend was really no laughing matter. *At all!*

Everyone else arrives at the office, and while we're going over my new sketches for the app, Ben is nowhere to be seen.

I call a morning meeting and tell them all about Kit's decision to pretty much keep my previous design but with the new color scheme he suggested. Charcoal and gold. Everyone seems genuinely happy, and they go about their day with cheerful attitudes. But when Ben arrives close to midday, the mood in the room drops to ice cold. Ben's eyes meet mine as he enters, but his gaze darts just as quickly.

"Where have you been?" I ask. "We've been going through the new design… It would have helped if you'd been here."

"Appointment," he says vaguely.

I know immediately that he's lying. I give him a doubtful look.

"Come on, Alex," Ben says tiredly. "We're colleagues here. It was an appointment, all right?"

Maybe he thinks I would never rat on him or get him fired, but right now, I'm moments away from doing something drastic.

"May I see you privately, Ben?"

He shrugs, knowing it's a demand and not a question.

All eyes are on us as I march him through to my private office at the back of the room. I shut the door, not giving Ben a chance to sit down before I begin laying in to him.

"Whatever your personal issues with me are, Ben, leave them outside of the office. First off you're late to a scheduled meeting, and now you are disrespecting me in front of my team. It's very unprofessional."

Ben laughs harshly. "I'm sorry, all right?"

I narrow my eyes at him, surprised by his chagrin.

"It's just that…" He shakes his head in frustration. "Why would you go for a guy like him when there's someone waiting right here who worships the ground you walk on? Why can't you see that he's just going to love you and leave you like he always does?"

"For the last time, I am not—"

"What does he have that I don't? I'm a good guy, Alex, and you have never once given me an opportunity to show you."

I'm suddenly furious. Who does he think he is?

"You know what, Ben? I think I know what your problem is. You're not nearly as nice as you think you are," I say calmly, trying to keep my voice level. "You tried to force yourself on me, and when I didn't feel the same, you decide to punish me by not showing up to work when you know I need your help and input on the relaunch. Somehow, Ben, I don't think I'm the problem. I think it's you."

He stares at me in silence for a long time.

I'm sweating in anger and frustration.

Ben finally turns his face away from me, his lips forming a grim line. Maybe I took it too far, but he had to be told.

I straighten up, adjusting my suit jacket and precede him to the door.

"I think we should get back to work now," I tell him quietly.

"Alex, wait," he says.

I turn around, giving him ten seconds.

"I'm sorry for what I did. I was jealous when I saw the way he looked at you and I wanted to stake a claim. And before you go off on me, Alex, please understand I was drunk out of my mind. So just…please believe, I am truly, genuinely sorry. I value your friendship. I value our working relationship. And I value you."

I look at him, taking in the regret in his eyes. "Much better," I say, softer now.

"It won't happen again, Alex," Ben says. "But I still think of you as my friend and I hope you do the same."

"Of course I do, Ben. I appreciate your friendship and I hope you know that it's valued."

He smiles sadly, then nods, and we leave my office.

I head to the coffee room, still restless about our encounter, only to hear, "Good morning, Alex," behind me as I prepare a cup for myself.

It's Kit. He's standing in the doorway, wearing a perfect suit.

"Good morning, Kit." I smile, suddenly remembering kissing that square jaw. It's not freshly shaven today. There's scruff along those hard planes, and it makes him look gorgeous.

He smiles lightly, scanning my features. "Have a good weekend?" He leans a shoulder on the doorframe.

"Lovely. Thank you. You?"

He nods, frowning as he continues regarding my expression. "Everything good here, Alex?"

I force myself to nod. "Of course. The usual stuff. Nothing to get concerned over." I won't rat Ben out to Kit. We've made peace now and I'm certain that he meant it.

"Good." Kit steps forward, reaches behind me for a cup and pours himself a coffee, covering it with a lid and setting it aside.

His nearness intoxicates me. I can't shake off the memory of the guy from Luciano's who teased me with an imaginary microphone. Even the guy who brought me lemonade after I got horribly drunk at his party.

"Your team aren't giving you trouble?" he persists.

"Nothing I can't take care of," I assure him. "I'm not always drunk and losing consciousness, you know."

His eyes twinkle. "Good to know."

"You know something else?" I tease.

One eyebrow slowly rises.

"The team is thrilled about the new design."

For a second, his eyes darken, as though he wanted me to say something else.

"Excellent news," he says, taking a sip of his coffee. "Ben just got in…?"

"I…" How did he know? "Yes, that's right."

"He didn't make it to today's meeting?" It's a statement disguised as a question.

"No." I won't lie to Kit, not for anything or anyone.

I'm shocked that he noticed. Then again, I'm quickly realizing that no mater how cool and easygoing Kit seems, he misses nothing.

"He said he had an appointment. It's all good."

"Glad to hear it. I'll talk to you about the design later, Ms. Croft."

"Okay, Mr. Walker." I answer in a mock formal tone, trying to keep things light.

But as I head for the door, I almost gasp to myself. *Was that jealousy I just saw in Kit's eyes?*

Fifteen

It's Thursday night when I get a text from Kit inviting me to dinner at his house on Friday to discuss work. Well, he calls it "work" but I've learned that nothing is that simple where Kit is concerned.

Of course, I can't go.

Not after our last evening out when it felt so much like…like more.

When I wanted *more*. When I kissed his cheek…and dreamed of him all night.

I'm insanely attracted to him, and I need to keep my walls up. So first thing in the morning, I will politely decline the offer. In person.

And *no*, I swear it's not just an excuse to see Kit.

After all, I'm uncomfortable and nervous about seeing him in person, and hate that I am because I rarely ever felt that way around Alastair.

But it's different…because it's *Kit*. This man has this way of pushing my buttons. *All of them.*

I arrive early at the office to more cheers from my co-workers who are still thrilled that I loosened up at the party last weekend. They've been doing this every day for the past week. They're such kids sometimes. Really.

"Go Alex!" Tim cheers when I arrive.

"Right, and we're still celebrating because…?"

"You let loose last weekend. Had some fun. Told off the big ole boss…" Tim adds, tongue in cheek.

"Don't remind me. Don't remind me *every day of my life.*" I roll my eyes, but inwardly laugh like they are laughing.

I head into my office to get some work done.

Kit never arrives until after nine o'clock. I wait until ten so I don't look too eager. Then I head to his office. I'm aware of Angela's eyes following me.

When I enter Kit's office, the first thing I notice is he's wearing glasses. Somehow, this shocks me. It makes him look more intelligent, if that's actually possible.

His face is screwed up in concentration as he clicks through some files on his computer. When he looks up at me, his eyes are magnified by the lenses.

Adorable.

I compose myself quickly, trying to push aside the thought that Kit has never looked better. "Morning, Kit."

"Hey, Alex. I was just reviewing some of the expenditure reports. Have you come to rescue me from boredom?"

I smile. "Actually… I just came to say I can't make it tonight."

Kit raises an eyebrow. "Big plans?"

"No… I'm just not sure I should. After last week. I don't want anyone at the office getting the wrong impression."

Kit doesn't seem concerned. "Come on, Alex. It's just a business dinner."

I blush. "I know but…our last business dinner was…"

More like a date to me, I think.

Kit takes off his glasses and stands up, coming around to my side of the desk.

A teasing light appears in his eyes. "As your boss, I demand that you come." He's obviously joking.

I smile slyly. "So fire me."

Kit rolls his eyes, but his lips twitch, even if he does seem a little exasperated. "We'll make it an early dinner. Just come for an hour."

"I don't think so…"

"Come on, Alex. You agreed to help mentor me. And I want to see the revised design. Am I to think you didn't really mean what you said? I won't take much of your time. What do you think?"

I waver.

I hate to admit it but being around Kit makes me feel totally vulnerable. Especially now that we are actually getting along. I can't deny my attraction to him anymore, and I don't want any office rumors to complicate things further.

My having dinner at his place will only add fuel to the fire. Even if it's only a business dinner.

There are a million reasons not to go. Probably more. But when it comes down to it, I want to spend more time with him. I *did* offer to mentor him, even if it means facing my shame and going back to that house. And I know that discussing business in a private place rather than a restaurant is more ideal—especially when trade secrets are going to be shared.

I sigh, and as the breath leaves my body, so does my resolve. "I guess an hour can't hurt…"

Kit grins smugly, returning to his chair. "I knew you'd come around."

"Yeah, well. I'm aiming to keep my job."

Kit smiles, picking up a pen and chewing the end. He's the perfect image of a schoolboy troublemaker. It's both endearing and totally inappropriate, but I decide I don't really care. I can appreciate him from afar, right?

"Just an hour, and I'm out. Deal?"

Kit's eyes sparkle. "Anything you want, Miss Croft." He releases a deep low male chuckle. "I'm just glad you're coming."

I nod and retreat from the office. I close the door behind me and take a deep breath. I guess I forgot to breathe for the entire meeting. I smile to myself as I return to my office. With the prospect of seeing Kit tonight, this day just got a whole lot better.

There's only so many times a girl can change her outfit without going insane.

I'm one dress change away from screaming right

now, with over ten options already lying discarded on the floor. I've spent longer getting ready than I plan to spend at Kit's place. I don't often look to others for validation, but all I want from this evening is for Kit to tell me I look good again.

This is ridiculous. It's a work dinner, not a hot date.

I guess he just wants me there to discuss business in private. Maybe after how receptive I was to him during our last dinner, he feels the best way to soften me up is with a good meal.

I groan as I check my watch. I'm due to arrive in half an hour, and it'll take me that long to get there. I snatch up a modest navy dress and throw it on. It'll have to do. At least it doesn't make me look tarty or desperate. The last thing I want is for my boss to think I'm dressing up for him. Even if I am.

I finish my hair and makeup in a hurry and leave the house without looking in the mirror. If I hesitate any more, I know I'll chicken out.

The whole drive, my heart keeps pace with the music on the radio, which is fast.

This doesn't feel like me. I'm not usually the kind of girl who gets frightened over work dinners.

Why did Kit have to turn out to be a good guy? With those looks of his, it's a killer combination, and it has complicated everything for me.

I kind of wish I could just go back to hating him, but in all honesty, this sensation I'm having right now is much more exciting.

When I pull up in his driveway, the first thing I notice is there's only one other vehicle parked there. A white Range Rover.

Kit's, I'm sure.

I wait in the car for a few minutes, half hoping he texts me and cancels, but he doesn't. I know he won't. Forcing myself to get out, I start walking to the front door.

Last time, the music was so loud I heard it from half-way down the road. Now it's so quiet and peaceful, like a whole different place.

I hesitate before knocking.

The thing is, I'm scared to be alone with him.

My feelings always seem to get more intense when I catch him alone.

It's in those moments when he is off guard. Softer. Better. It's those moments where I find myself drawn to him like a magnet.

It's such an alien feeling to me that I hardly know what to do with it.

Exhaling, I prod myself to move. I can't just stand here all night. So before I can stop myself, I knock on the door.

I wait, but there's no response. I'm starting to feel like this whole thing is a prank. Everyone at work will be laughing at me when they find out.

When nobody answers, I start to fume. I'm totally being pranked. I shake my head in frustration, wishing I could just go home. But something keeps me glued to the doorstep. I'm confused. Intrigued.

Why would Kit ask me here and not open? I'm sure

he's not above playing practical jokes, but why now? Why me, when we are finally on track?

Maybe he's trying to stir things up again, but somehow, that doesn't feel like a viable explanation.

I'm about to turn away when it occurs to me to try the doorknob. When I turn it, the door clicks, opening slowly. My heart gives a little kick of anticipation as I step inside, flustered by this entire thing. Then I glance around and see something amazing.

The entire room is filled with black roses.

Sixteen

I stare in awe at the mind-blowing floral display before me, my chest almost collapsing in on itself from the shock. I walk slowly to the vase closest to me, stroking the petals of a long black rose gently. They're real. *This* is real. I look up and catch sight of my face in the mirror.

Any resolve I had before I walked in here starts melting away. This sexy man is playing my heart like a guitar, and all I want is for him to keep up this insane melody.

When I turn, he's waiting for me. He's dressed in a black suit, his hair wet from a recent bath. His jaw is clenched, and though he's standing with his feet braced apart and his arms crossed, he gives off an air of restlessness. As if he doesn't know how this is going to go.

My heart melts right along with the rest of me. It seems I'm the not only person coming undone.

"I'm glad you could make it," Kit finally says, a muscle working in the back of his jaw as he holds my gaze. He seems to be thinking about what to say.

I stare around the room, still unable to believe he went to all this trouble.

"Kit…what's the occasion?"

He exhales, then looks around. "Turns out, black roses…*natural* black roses…only grow in this village in Turkey. So it took some time to bring them in." When his eyes meet mine, they're bright with emotion. He walks slowly toward me, a smile playing on his lips. "I felt like setting the creative tone for the evening, to celebrate your vision."

I don't reply. My heart is racing and I'm light-headed. This doesn't feel real. The smell of the roses is so strong that I feel like I've died and gone to flower heaven. But this is too much. I'm not sure that I'm ready.

Kit stops only inches away from me. He smells a little sweaty, like the anticipation of this moment has got him all riled up. What happened to Mr. Calm, Cool and Collected? Then again, I'm not exactly a portrait of composure; right now, my legs are actually trembling.

"I want you," he tells me quietly.

My voice isn't my own. It's too breathy, too vulnerable. "I want you, too," I manage to whisper. This is what he's made me. This is what he's done to me.

Nostrils flaring as if my admission does something to him, he runs a finger from my eyebrows, down my cheek, to my chin. It rests there for a moment before continuing its journey down my neck.

As he reaches my collarbone, he brushes aside the

strap of my dress and presses his lips to the skin beneath it. It's agonizing. He's kissing everywhere but my lips. But I don't want him to stop. My whole body clutches in yearning, and my skin burns under every spot his lips touch.

His lips trail to my jaw, tiny kisses like whispers caressing my skin.

His hands find my hips and I want to crush my body against him. But I hold back because I sense that this moment is far too tender. I'm scared if I move, everything we're sharing will shatter, like waking up from a beautiful dream.

I need to get this out of my system. I need to get *him* out of my system. I cup my hand around his neck, drawing his face closer to mine. We stay close, but not touching for a few moments, the only sound in the air that of our heavy breathing.

"Kit...why did you do all this?" I ask. I don't want to break the moment, but I have to know.

Kit's nose nudges mine so that I'm forced to look at him. "I wanted to do something special for you. Have a moment alone with you. And... I really needed to see you."

My stomach dips pleasantly and I can't help but smile. Kit caresses my cheeks as he continues. "I know we didn't have the best start, but this whole time..."

"I know," I whisper. I know because I felt it, too. As crazy as this is, it's starting to feel like it was meant to be.

When his lips cover mine, I sigh into his mouth, our bodies finally finding any way possible to touch.

He presses me hard against the door, his hands exploring every inch of me. His tongue flicks relentlessly over mine, first coaxingly, then faster and more demanding as I open wider to him and let him have it. Let him have *me*.

Kit hooks a hand under my knee and pulls it up, so my leg is curled around his hips. He nips my ear with his teeth and I gasp, melting further into him. He stops for a moment and we make eye contact. We're frozen in time, staring at one another. The whole world seems to recede; it's only him. I try to recall sex with my other partners. Did it ever feel this way?

Never.

"It's a beautiful night…" Kit whispers, his nose nudging mine again. "Shall we go outside?"

I nod, still dazed. Kit's movements become gentle again. I unhook myself from him, missing his body against mine the moment we part.

He wants me, I keep thinking. Dazed. Amazed. And wanting—no, *aching*—for him, too.

Quietly, Kit takes my hand in his and guides me through the house. Fresh June air hits my sweaty skin and I can't help feeling relieved. I get the feeling things are about to get much hotter anyway.

The sun is beginning to set, reflecting on the pool. It's the romantic setting I never imagined being in. Kit turns to me, his eyes bright. He lets go of my hand, backing himself up to sit on a lounger. He beckons me with one finger as he lies back, his member bulging against his pants. But I want to be in control. He might be my boss at work, but here, even in his territory, it's a different story.

I shake my head.

He watches in curiosity as I step out of my shoes, taking baby steps in his direction. I allow my hand to gently run up the length of my body. I touch my face. My breasts. My legs. My right hand trails up the back of my dress and finds the zipper, slowly pulling it down. Kit watches with his lips slightly parted, his eyes darting all over my body. He doesn't know where to look.

I smile to myself. I'll show him where to look.

I push the dress from my shoulders and let it fall away from me. Now I'm standing there in nothing but a black thong. I hear the intake of his breath as my fingers dance around the lace underwear, slowly dipping underneath the material to tease myself.

From years of bad dates and allowing unworthy men into my life, I've learned to pleasure myself the way I deserve. I'm already wet as my fingers part my sex, nudging my clit as I begin to take the pleasure I've waited so long for. Kit fixes me in his gaze as he removes his jacket and shirt, his shoes already discarded beside him. I move closer, ready to let him have a role.

I straddle him with my hand still buried between my legs. Then I dip myself down to grind up against him, making him moan. One of his hands works on my breasts, his thumb and forefinger pinching my nipples, while his other hand guides my hips, working up a rhythm. Our eyes meet and I decide to give him a show he'll enjoy. I bite my lip with a knowing smile, increasing my pace against him. He looks a little surprised at my ferocity, but not disappointed. He swoops in for a kiss, my eyes closing in bliss as my lips part.

Suddenly, he's flipped me onto my back before I can protest. He looks smug as he kisses my chest, making his way down my body.

"I can't let you do all the hard work," he murmurs. Giving me a wolfish smile as he raises his amber gaze, his teeth clamp on the string of my thong, tugging it down my legs.

In the process, he exposes my hand, my fingers still working on my clit. As my thong reaches my ankles I kick it off, giving Kit a clear path. He nudges my legs apart, kissing my thighs. My breathing quickens in anticipation. I know what's coming, my body clutching in want.

Kit's tongue is warm as he runs it along my sex. I close my eyes, soaking up the attention. He nudges my clit and a shiver runs down my spine, a moan escaping me. It only brings him closer, his hands holding my hips in place as he sets a deeper kiss on me, licking and kissing me between my legs. I'm unused to this intimacy with another person, but I love it. I clench my legs along the sides of his head, pulling him in closer, but he doesn't complain. The movements of his tongue seem to become even more skilled and fierce as he continues, his fingers possessively digging into my hipbones.

Before I know it, he's sent me over the edge. My first orgasm overcomes me and I moan, tilting my head back to enjoy the moment. But Kit doesn't give me much time to recover. I hear his belt drop with a clatter and feel myself tremble again as he stands, looming above me.

I reach out. My hands shake as I loosen his shirt from the waistband of his slacks. "I want you," I rasp. He helps me tug open the rest of his shirt buttons and shrugs off his shirt. I admire his glorious physique for a moment and then lean forward to lick one nipple. Playfully, first. More hungrily after hearing him groan deep in his throat.

He seems desperate as he pulls off his pants and his boxers, revealing his impressive length.

I lick my lips as he positions himself between my thighs. No longer playing. Both of us too eager for the other. He twines one of my legs around his hips and pins one of my hands at my side, then works on a condom with his free hand. When he enters me, I moan. I moan again when he withdraws, and moan harder when he returns.

"Kit," I gasp.

"That's right, Alex. My beautiful, strong Alex, who is it that you want?"

"You."

My free hand wanders over his back, my nails leaving claw marks as our pace quickens. My pinned hand clenches and unclenches with each of his delicious thrusts.

I realize very quickly Kit is expert at this. He drives into me like he can't get enough, watching me take him with moan after moan. His eyes flash as my own gaze blurs from the pleasure. His pace is relentless, powerful, dominating.

I see stars when I'm overtaken by a second orgasm. This time I explode so hard I'm crying his name. I don't even realize I do it. He groans my name in return, ducking his head close to my ear, voice raw and quiet. In that moment my name sounds hotter than I ever imagined it could sound.

I spread myself wider to give him space and Kit continues to sink into me. It's as if he never wants to stop being inside me. I gasp each time he enters me. He's not being slow and gentle. He's moving like he needs me right this second. He kisses me with equal fervor. I'm not complaining one bit. He releases my wrist and tugs gently at my hair, his grip on me tight, but forgiving. He's rough as he kisses me, but in a good way. I don't ever want him to let me go, to stop giving me these fiercely, violently tender kisses. I stare up at the evening sky and the last rays of sunlight that streak across its horizon. Kit's face is cast in their glow as he eases back to meet my gaze again. His expression is tight with passion, eyes bright gold and beautiful, and I want him, I want all of him. I push him to his back and suddenly lower myself onto him. Impaling myself. Kit's muscular body is now beneath me, and I'm riding him. Shamelessly.

He clenches his jaw and his eyes blaze bright as he cups my breasts, which bounce with my movements. Then he grabs my pelvis and thrusts upward at the same time he pulls me downward.

We're staring at each other as if nothing else exists. Kit's eyes continue getting shinier but darker, his eyelids half-mast, his pupils dilated. A low groan rumbles up from his chest, his hands clenching on my hipbones as he drives up and goes off.

He's beautiful at this moment, shrouded in sweat, his face tight in passion as he pulls me deeper down onto him. As he rocks back and forth during his orgasm, I close my eyes, feeling him feel me, riding him to oblivion as my body starts tightening again. I'm surprised when he reaches between our bodies to flick my clit with his thumb, and suddenly the touch, coupled with the passion of our lovemaking, sends me off a third time.

When I finally open my eyes, Kit's chest is glistening with sweat, rising and falling with his breaths. His hands are still on my hips. Possessive. Strong and gentle at the same time. He has this gorgeous smile on his face.

He's still inside me, our bodies still one.

My heart hurts in my chest while simultaneously it feels like it's flying somewhere in the heavens. In this moment, that elusive perfect design that every designer craves—perfect on the inside, on the outside, all around—that's us. *We* are a perfect design.

Moments later, Kit shifts me around and lowers me to his side, withdrawing but keeping me flush with him. His arm remains protectively around my shoulders and pins me close.

I don't want him to let go of me, and I'm surprised by how hard I cling to his shoulder so that he doesn't.

"Shame on me," Kit rasps softly, a dark brown curl falling over his forehead as he looks down at me. He sounds apologetic, but his smile is very male and satisfied. "You deserve a bed, Miss Croft."

"I don't want a bed. But if you insist." I groan and

stretch a little in his arms. I feel so good. The way Kit regards me makes me feel even better. I stroke my fingers lovingly along his hard shoulders.

"Come along, then. Let's get you inside." He scoops me up as if I were a little girl and I giggle as he dips me to the ground so I can pick up our clothes. "Want to bring that along?" he asks.

"It might come in handy later," I tease as I quickly pull our clothes into my arms and bundle them all together in a ball. Kit carries me into his mansion.

"How gentlemanly."

I leave our clothes on my lap and I link my fingers behind his strong neck. I can't remember when I've ever felt this pampered—or cherished.

Never, Alex.

The thought that I've never felt this happy confuses me. The feelings I'm experiencing are so strong that I don't even know what to call them. Nervousness and guilt over what I just did with the boss is there. And yet, even stronger than that, there's another feeling. And that is freedom. The kind I've never felt before.

"There are many things you don't know about me," Kit huskily warns as he looks down at me with a playful expression. "That you need to learn firsthand rather than picking it up from office gossip."

"Like what?"

"Like…" He pauses, his forehead scrunching as he considers it. "I'm chivalrous."

"Are you sure?" I fake disbelief. "How come this has never come up in the office gossip before?"

A smirk touches his lips. "I just hadn't found the right lady to bring out this trait in me."

"Aha." I laugh.

He brings me to the kitchen and sets me down on one of the stools lined up at the counter. He takes our clothes and sets them on the sofa in the adjacent living room and then disappears. He returns wearing black silk pajama bottoms and offers me a white terry bathrobe to slip into.

I stand and cover my nakedness with the robe. As I knot the sash around my waist, I pad into the kitchen and try to at least pretend I'm not staring at his athletic form and the way his chest and muscles ripple as he moves around, pulling out glasses and flatware for us. "What's this about?" I ask.

"I won't ask you to dinner and leave you hungry." He pulls out a bottle of white wine that's been chilling in the refrigerator.

"My, my, you cook?" I tap the corner of my mouth in interest and eye the bottle of wine he presents. I'm impressed by his choice.

"No." He grins as he extracts two covered plates from the hot drawer next to the fridge. "But I have excellent skills in hiring the best cooks around."

Eyes twinkling playfully, he jerks his chin in the direction of the dining table. A silent command for me to sit there. I take a seat, and Kit sets the plates on the table, then takes the chair at the head, next to me.

He pours the wine. We have the most delicious pasta for dinner. I find myself laughing and sending sultry glances his way over the rim of my wineglass. Why does this boy bring out the flirt in me? No. Not boy. He's a man, the most attractive one I've ever known.

I feel so relaxed, I could stay here with Kit in his mansion forever. But a pang reverberates in my heart because I know I can't. This is just a stolen moment—and it won't last.

Not with him.

I still relish it, though.

Kit makes me laugh. And I realize as we talk about Cupid's Arrow and his plans for the company that I admire him. That I may have even misjudged him. True, he is more relaxed than I am, but underneath the casual attitude and party boy facade lie a sharp mind and a kind heart. I even like his sense of humor. The way that lock of dark hair falls over his eyes. The way he's shown respect for me. Even the way he is with his father. I bet he would make a good father himself one day. I'm surprised I even think that. But the image of a gorgeous little Kit toddling around makes me smile.

"Fess up, Miss Croft. What's that smile all about?"

I choke on a laugh—there's no way I'd tell him what I was just thinking. Instead, I say, "You're very surprising, Mr. Walker. Seems you're on your way to mending your wicked ways at the tender age of…?"

"Twenty-seven."

"Ah." I nod over this revelation.

"Ah, what?"

"I'm twenty-four. But I'm way ahead of you in experience." I wave his age off as if it doesn't mean anything.

Kit leans forward and challenges me with a sharp glance, his voice deep and suggestive. "Work experience, maybe. Life, I'm not so sure, Alex. Sexually I'm certain I've got decades on you, pussycat."

"Kit Walker! You can't complain about what happened just now." An alien blush creeps up my neck as I speak those words and it seems to bring out Kit's mischievous smile again.

He slowly shakes his head. "Not one bit. Except…" he trails off.

"Except what?"

His voice drops a decibel. "I'm not done with you, Miss Croft." He reaches out to squeeze my hand over the table before he pours us some more wine.

I don't know why, but I'm restless as we finish dinner now. Eager to feel his hands on me again. To come undone for this man—my boss—again.

Kit carries the plates to the sink. And before I can even look at my clothes piled up on his fine living room couch, he links his fingers with mine and leads me up to his bedroom.

Seventeen

I wake up alone in a big bed and glance around, taking two seconds to recognize where I am. *Kit's room.* And suddenly what we did last night comes back to me.

Smiling, I ease out of bed and hop into the shower and spending five minutes fantasizing about last night while I'm soaping and shampooing myself. Then I step out and wrap up in a towel.

Spotting my clothes neatly folded on the nightstand, I quickly get dressed and snatch up my heels.

I pad downstairs, dressed but barefoot. I spot Kit bent over a laptop in the living room. My heart skips a beat at the sight of his disheveled dark brown hair. I ache to run my fingers through the curls at his nape.

He's bare chested, wearing nothing but slacks, his hair fresh from a recent shower.

I could have died and gone to heaven. But I know from the fast beat of my heart that I'm very much alive. Very. Much. Alive.

And very much into the wicked temptation that is Kit Walker.

Oh, what to do. What to *do*?

I really don't want to overstay my welcome.

He glances up from his laptop, a smile curving his lips.

"Good morning, Miss Croft." Kit stands and sets his laptop aside. "Are you hungry? I guess it's almost lunchtime…" he says, his gaze raking me appreciatively head to toe.

Feeling myself blush and not yet ready to go as well as sensing that he isn't ready to let me go yet either, I set my heels aside. "Good morning, Mr. Walker. Yes. I actually am. I could cook something for us. Soup maybe?"

"Sounds good."

I try not to stare at his bare chest while I make myself busy collecting ingredients from the fridge.

I lay everything out, trying to stay calm. I'm happy that I found enough goodies to make a decent vegetable soup.

Kit crosses the room, peering around me inquisitively.

"You seem nervous. Why?" His voice is a low, gruff whisper fluttering the hairs at the top of my head.

I shake my head first, then nod, confirming his suspicion. How do I tell him that I can't stop thinking about him? That I want him more than I've wanted anything in my life?

I can't.

I still can't really fully admit it to myself. "I guess I don't know what's going on here."

Kit bites his lip, then releases it. "Yeah. Me neither. But there's no use hiding away from it, right?"

I shrug shyly. "I guess not."

"There's a lot I have to tell you… I want us to have the final design worked out and take the app for a test drive next week. Get everyone in the office to open a profile, check out the messaging system…"

I shift positions to face him, alert. "I love that idea!"

I'm so excited, I feel heat rushing through me, and I smile as the warmth reaches my cheeks.

I stare at Kit. "I can't believe we never thought about doing a double beta before…"

"I know…this'll help us relaunch to the public with more confidence. And avoid any pitfalls."

"I'm so excited."

"Me too." Kit pulls me in for a hug, and I let him.

I let him because I need someone to help me believe that this is actually happening. That this is really my life. I know maybe it shouldn't be my boss, the one whose embrace I crave most.

And yet here I am, unable to pull away. Kit Walker is holding me in his strong arms, and I really want it to be real. Kit strokes the back of my head.

Both of us smile as I ease back and look up at him.

"We can download it now. I was going to share the news last night before we got caught up in something just as good." His eyes twinkle.

"It's really ready to download?"

"Certainly." He pulls out his phone. "I've got it right here. We still need to change the design, but most of the tech side is done. Here. I'm texting you the link."

I fish out my phone, click the link in his text and download the app.

By the time it downloads, we're teasing each other and setting up our profiles. Kit just uses KW, so I go with AC.

"Send me a heart," he instructs as we navigate.

I send him a heart.

Suddenly, my app pings back.

KW sent you a heart.

I smile.

"Now send me a message," Kit instructs.

I shoot him a simple one. Just one word.

Testing

Kit reads my message, his eyebrows pulling together thoughtfully as if he expected something else. He smiles wryly at some sort of private joke only he knows, and tucks his phone away. "We'll get the beta test done and then go live once we work out the kinks," he tells me.

I'm grinning ear to ear, forcing myself to tuck my phone away, too. "I can't wait."

I return to the counter to get back to work on the soup.

I'm really glad that I never reported anything negative about Kit to Alastair. It's all going well. We may not know what's going on between us, but we're consenting adults, and as long as we keep it strictly business in the office, maybe we can figure it out.

My heart jumps happily at the thought.

I head over to the sink to wash the vegetables and Kit follows me. He watches as if he's never seen a woman cook before. "I usually make this when I'm sick."

"Where did you learn to cook? Your parents? Mum never cooked for me, and Alastair is hopeless."

I laugh. "Who cooked for you? Your nanny?" When he nods, I determine to cook for this man whenever possible. "Like I told you, my parents are the most dedicated workaholics you'll ever meet. But even though they've worked most of their lives, there wasn't always a lot of money to pay for nannies. They're compulsive business starters. So that left me in charge of my sister Helena while we grew up. Unfortunately, I'm not a very good cook. But I tried, at least. I sort of taught myself to cook her healthy things." I glance at him over my shoulder. "Did your brother never cook for you, either?"

"Not really. We're not that close. Plus, William's an uptight perfectionist, and although I know he can cook, I doubt he'd ever cook for anyone. He's such a hard-ass, people nicknamed him Stone. He can't stand anything but working and living by the rules. Me?" He cants his head sideways. "I bloody love breaking rules. It drives him up the wall."

I laugh. "You two sound like complete opposites."

"We're vastly different," Kit concedes. "His mum is a socialite. My mum... Dad met her at Platinum. A strip club in London." A wry smile touches his lips but it doesn't conceal the love he feels for her in his eyes.

I'd never spoken to anyone so openly about my family. I can sense Kit doesn't open up about the subject, either.

There's an intimacy between us in this moment that wasn't there before.

An unspoken truce. Even *more* than that, something like open respect and admiration.

It's as if overnight, we founded each other's fan club.

"Sometimes I overwork myself," I confide. "I used to think it was a good thing, but seeing my parents take it too far my whole life…and also after meeting you… I don't know. Until now, it's been scary because I had no one to stop me, and I rarely stop myself because of my sister, Helena."

"What about Helena?"

"I pay for her studies. My parents encouraged us to make our own way after high school. They think people don't put their best foot forward unless they're pressured to do so. But Helena's my sister, and I want to offer her every opportunity possible so that when her time comes, she will go out there and succeed. I guess that's why I'm a workaholic, too. I can't help it, I was raised to be one, and it's in my DNA." I smirk. "You haven't been around long enough to see me work myself into a perennial state of insomnia during a big launch."

"Really, Alexandra?" Kit *tsks* quietly. "We can't have that, beautiful. It seems that my father and I have been working you too hard at the office."

The protectiveness in his eyes makes me blush, and

I almost want to put my walls back up. I'm not used to being so vulnerable around anyone. It feels good opening up. But maybe too good.

"Hey, I love it. Don't take it *too* easy on me or treat me like I'm fragile or I'll get mad. You won't like me mad." I smirk and stick my tongue out at him playfully.

Kit laughs. "My little redhead, spitting fire."

He's teasing me, nuzzling my ear as he does.

I smile shyly at his use of the word *my*, ducking my head under his arm to get out the plates.

"You know, I owed you some soup since the day you brought me your mom's lemonade. I think that's the day I realized I liked you more than I wanted to."

I blush for a moment, realizing what I've just admitted out loud.

"I didn't bring you lemonade so you would make me soup, Alex."

My teasing smile falters at the somberness in his tone.

"I know," I admit, turning to face him. "You were nice to me that day. I remember seeing you at that door and thinking, 'damn, he's here to gloat.' But you weren't. You were actually trying to help me feel better. It was noble of you. One of the many things I've grown to admire and…appreciate about you."

Love about you, a shocking little whisper in my subconscious pipes in.

Kit is silent for a moment, watching me. Then he changes the subject. "You look sexy when you cook…" His voice is getting huskier, and my heart is pounding harder.

I try to play it cool, though his simple touch has

sent me into overdrive. "I'm just chopping veggies…"
I waggle my knife at him. "So, that's your kink, hmm?
A bit of knife play?"

Kit hoists himself onto the counter next to me.

I smile, but I'm a little distracted by how close he
is. His leg is practically touching me. He reaches out
and brushes a hair behind my ear. "Maybe I'm just into
anything you do."

I coyly duck away from his hand, continuing to chop
the vegetables.

Kit hops down from the counter, his hands moving
straight to my waist. I drop the knife on the counter,
letting out a little gasp as his face comes close to mine.
My heart is racing. Everything is moving so quickly but
I don't mind. My eyes flicker to his lips.

Then I'm kissing him, desperately, my hands claw-
ing for every part of him I can reach. We stumble together, a mess of limbs, and I feel alive again. I allow
myself to forget everything that's happened lately as I
lose myself in his touch.

Kit pulls away to look at me. "Is this okay?" he
gruffs out.

I pull him back to me, nodding frantically. "This is
what I've been waiting for."

He tugs me closer and I kiss him back with abandon. With my whole *being*. Then I pull out one of the
kitchen chairs and push him down on it. I clamber on
top of him, and Kit smiles, letting me take the reins. I
push my breasts up against his face as I make myself
comfortable.

He leans forward and kisses me harder, his hunger matching mine.

I'm losing control, but I don't want control anymore. I just want him.

I grind against his erection. I can feel how wet I've become in a short amount of time, desperate to get intimate with Kit. Feel him inside me again. Move with him, come apart for him. With him.

His hands grip my ass hard, guiding me as I move against him. He groans, and loosens the sash of the terry bathrobe he loaned me. He parts and eases it down my shoulders, and his hungry lips find my bare breasts, his tongue warm and soft as it explores my skin. I can't help letting out a whimper, the robe sliding to my feet. He pauses to run his hands over me, examining every inch of me with hungry eyes.

"God, Alex…" he murmurs, his lips dipping back to my skin. His touch is delicate and sweet, like he's making love for the first time. But right now, that's not what I need.

"You don't have to be gentle with me," I breathe.

Kit's eyes meet mine.

He flashes me a wicked grin, and I shiver in anticipation, closing my eyes and moving faster against him. I know I'm soaked, but I don't care. I'm not embarrassed to admit that I find him so very hot.

Kit suddenly lifts me up off his lap, placing me on the table. He takes off his slacks, and I don't know what to do with myself, so I lay back slightly on my elbows. The maneuver is awkward, reminding me of my college days and the few times I slept with a guy. But when Kit pushes my legs apart, I know this won't be anything like that.

I frantically wrap my legs around him, pulling him in for a kiss. Then he's carrying me again, leading us out of the kitchen and up the stairs.

In his room, I feel a sense of nostalgia, and a hint of regret for when I need to leave here. I've secretly dreamed for nights about his kiss, his hands on me. Now I'm here, and I'm making the memory I've been aching for. Again. But it feels too good to be true.

We fall onto the bed together. I can feel his cock pressing against me as he moves between my legs slowly, teasing me.

"I won't last if you keep doing that," I tell him. He gives me a sly smile, his dark eyes full of mischief.

"Say please."

I scowl, taking matters into my own hands. I push him away from me. Kit doesn't protest as I clamber on top of him, his hands immediately moving to grasp my breasts.

"So, this is how it's going to be…"

I nod cheekily.

Kit watches me, lust in his eyes. He sits up and slides a finger inside me. It was a move that I wasn't expecting, but one I can't claim to dislike. I buck against him. Our eyes meet as his pace quickens, and he slides two more fingers inside me. I grip his hair hard, pulling his hand away from my wetness and to his lips. He sucks his fingers gently, his eyes fixated on mine. He seems almost in a trance, mesmerized by what's happening.

I place a hand on Kit's chest, pushing him back down

again. I'm done waiting. I want the main event. "Condoms?" I ask breathily.

He stretches out his arm and pulls out a packet from his nightstand. He tears it open, and I grab the rubber, loving the way he groans when I slide it on him. I position myself over him, stroking his penis gently. He shivers, his eyes never leaving mine.

"I expected to be doing a bit more of the heavy lifting..."

I smile down at him. Towering over him, naked, I feel glorious. I feel myself. "You'll get your chance later."

Before Kit can say anything, I sink down on his hard length. He moans in pleasure as I work up a rhythm. It's been a long time since I did something so raw and sexual, but I find it comes to me naturally. With him, I knew it would.

Each time, I sink down on him a little farther, pushing him deeper and deeper inside me. He sits up to guide me, his lips exploring my body and his hands supporting my ass. I'm sweating, breathless, but alive.

More alive than I have been for a long time.

"You feel so good," I gasp, clutching the back of his head closer to my breasts while Kit hungrily suckles me. "Please don't stop," I rasp in his ear. "I want you. Please."

"Shh. Alex...if you want me, you'll have me." His tone is almost amused as he rolls me onto my back. And when he pins my hands above my head and thrusts again, I see stars. Giving up complete control, giving myself to him.

"Kit!" I cry with every ramming of his hips, gripping his hands with mine, which he keeps pinned down to the bed. His erection fills me up so completely I feel stretched and possessed by this man. This fantasy.

He groans, thrusting harder as his breathing grows more rapid. "You feel good, Alex, so damn good…" Our pace becomes crazy and jerkier as we approach our climax, and then we're there. His name leaves my lips on a moan as I hear him groan out "Alex" in a way that pushes me even farther past the edge.

When it's over, Kit and I lie in bed. My legs are trembling.

"I feel like with all these distractions, I should give up on making the soup."

Kit nuzzles my neck. "Totally worth it." His lips find mine again, and I close my eyes, sighing into him.

Eighteen

I haven't stopped thinking about him. Not for a second since I drove back home Sunday afternoon. Not when I climbed into my own bed for a nap and remembered everything we did and said, every touch and look.

Alastair messages me Sunday evening.

Alex. Can you provide a quick update?

I read his text and sigh, wishing I could simply ignore it but knowing that's the last thing I should do. I don't want to be telling on Kit. I'm falling for him. I've grown to admire his business sense. But what we're doing together probably wouldn't go over well with Alastair. At all. I feel like an awful person, and I don't want to deal with it.

But I can't deny that he's still the top dog—even if semiretired. And that I have Helena and her studies to think about, too. So I dial him up and give him the briefest debriefing possible. That Kit gave me some markups on the new design and we've been applying the changes.

"So his suggestions were to your liking?" Alastair asks, sounding pleased.

"Very much. We're taking it out on a test run this week after Kit gives his final approval of the design," I say.

"Excellent! Excellent!" Alastair sounds very pleased. "I knew you'd pull through for me, Alex. I know he's a tough one to handle but you can do it."

"He's…stubborn, yes. But not entirely hopeless," I admit, smiling fondly as I think of him.

"Good. Anything else?"

"Nothing at all," I quickly say.

There's a silence, then Alastair says, "Right. Oh, and Alex?"

"Yes?"

"There was a reason you were always my favorite. I know I can always count on you."

"Thank you, Alastair."

I hang up with a pain in my chest. I'm such a fraud. I'm betraying Alastair's trust, sleeping with Kit. I'm betraying my own sense of what's right. I'm becoming one of Kit's groupies. I can't help but wonder if I'm going to regret what happened…but how can I when every inch of me burns with yearning for it to happen again?

I'm nervous when I arrive at work on Monday. Kit needs to approve the final design, and I don't know what will happen when we see each other. Was it a one-night stand? Has he been thinking about me the way I've been thinking about him?

I try to push my personal feelings and concerns out of my mind as I arrive. After I set down my purse and portfolio, I clap to get everyone's attention. "Good morning. Kit is stopping by today to approve the final design. Let's take a look at it, shall we?"

We gather around the long table. "Is Ben here yet? I called the meeting—"

"I'm here," Ben calls from the door, walking forward with a smile.

I return the smile with one of my own, grateful that we can move forward from what happened.

Ellie sidles up besides me. "Did something happen?" Her voice is low, only loud enough for me to hear.

I pretend to be surprised. "Why do you ask that?"

She taps a finger to the corner of her lips as a smile appears. "Only because you blushed when you said Kit's name. And you never returned my messages this weekend."

"You're hallucinating. I was busy getting this ready," I mutter, briskly grabbing the wall screen remote to display the final design.

I'm dying to talk to someone—anyone—about what happened at Kit's place this weekend. But a part of me is still too cautious about this whole thing to want to get my hopes up. And another part of me is rather concerned that I'm developing feelings for my boss. I've slept with my boss.

I never thought I'd ever be this kind of girl.

I'm trying to measure how much to tell Ellie when there's a wave of restlessness in the room.

"Good morning."

My head snaps up at the sound of Kit's low masculine baritone. He heads into the room while Angela titters and the team shuffles excitedly around the table.

He looks…edible. Black suit. Perfectly knotted tie. I can't believe this is the same guy I met only mere weeks ago. He looks like the real deal.

"Good morning. Miss Croft." His amber eyes meet mine, and my breath goes short.

Because in that piercingly intimate gaze I can see every bit of what I did, what *we* did together reflected back at me.

"I trust you all had a good weekend." Kit looks around at my team, but I sense he's directing the question to me.

"A marvelous one, actually," I reply in my most businesslike tone. "We're starting off the week with good news—the new design is ready for you to approve."

Kit comes to stand next to me while I motion toward the final design.

We're keeping the same font we used previously, but we've added an actual double arrow on the last letter— the *W*—of *Cupid's Arrow*. The double arrow means that not only was Cupid busy shooting his arrow at one person—but both actually felt the sting.

I can't help but wonder if that's what's happening here.

I feel Kit's body heat; he's standing so close, our shoulders are almost touching.

Kit shifts back and crosses his arms as he runs his eyes over every inch of the wall screen. The charcoal background and shimmering gold lettering really pack a punch. The design looks timeless, elegant.

"I added the arrows last minute. Do you like that?" I ask.

"I do. I like what I see. Very much." Kit turns and fixes his gaze on me. "Excellent job." It takes him a moment to direct his gaze to each of my team members next, repeating his praise.

The relief at his words is suddenly palpable in the air. For the next half hour, we discuss beta testing, launch plans and navigational details we'll need Ben to sort out.

Once the meeting is done, Kit reaches out and seizes my hand at my side, gently squeezing. "Well done." I blink and glance up at the others. Praying that nobody noticed. I exhale nervously when I realize most of them did.

"Walk with me to the elevators?" Kit asks as he turns to leave.

I nod briskly, aware of Ben hovering nearby. Is he following us?

"See you tonight at my place," Kit says as he pushes the up arrow, turns and smiles down at me. My heart leaps in joy.

My eyes widen when I realize Ben has overheard. "Yes, tonight, for ah, our business dinner…?"

Kit nods, and I smile and watch him board the elevator, my heart thudding faster and faster at the prospect of seeing him again.

Ben clears his throat. "So I guess you're friends now?"

"Yes. It's a good thing. We should all get along."

"Of course." His expression is friendly, and I'm once again glad we've been able to move past what happened.

That was easily resolved. I just wish what's going on with Kit and me was as easy to figure out.

I'm all abuzz as I work from my private office. I can't help it, but every time I remember Kit's invitation, my body tingles a little more. I try to focus on sending the design files to the tech department so they can get everything ready for the launch.

At three o'clock, when I haven't heard anything else from Kit, I decide to send him a text to fish out some info about tonight.

What's the plan for tonight? When/where should we meet? I type nervously.

My place? 7ish? Bring your swimsuit. Or nothing at all ;)

You are too forward, Mr. Walker.

A guy can hope, Ms. Croft.

I grin and push my phone back into my bag, anticipation making the rest of the day go by fast.

That night at my place, after I shower, I apply my most delicious-smelling pear and vanilla cream all over my body. Then I grab my swimsuit and pack it into a small duffel. I wonder if I should pack my pajamas, too. No. No way, Alexandra Croft. It would be too obvious. You still don't even know what's going on.

I quickly blow dry my hair and comb it in a loose style, then put on a simple but flirty white sundress. Satisfied that I look good and determined not to overthink this, I lock up my apartment and head to Kit's place.

Kit is on the phone when I arrive. He's still in his slacks and white button-down shirt, his jacket discarded on the back of the living room sofa. Kit spots me as I peer inside, his eyes flaring at the sight of me.

Yep. I'm glad I went for the white dress.

"Dad, I've got to go," Kit murmurs into the phone, motioning me forward. "Something's come up. I'm glad you like what we've done so far."

Alastair seems to ask something that makes Kit bring the phone closer to his ear. "Miss Croft?" Brows slowly rising, Kit eyes me leisurely, his gaze trekking up and down my body. "We're getting along splendidly."

He smiles and hangs up.

"Hey there." He approaches almost tentatively, as if shy about this whole thing. He shoves his hands into his pockets, smiling down at me. "Shall we hit the pool?"

"I'm up for that. Is there somewhere I can change?"

"Guest bedroom. The pool cabana. Or…my room."

Again his smile is almost nervous, but mischievous enough that I'm nervous, too.

"Pool cabana is fine." I carry my duffel outside and walk into the cabana, changing into a little black bikini with red ribbon ties. I eye myself in the mirror for a whole three minutes.

"Okay, Alex. Relax. It's not a life or death situation here. Just go out there and have a good time," I say to myself. So why does it feel like it's a life or death situation?

Because he's my boss?

And the son of my boss?

Maybe we should talk about this.

I step out, blinking against the setting sun. Kit is on a lounger, his gorgeous bare chest on display, a pair of turquoise swim trunks hugging his lean hips and waist. His hair is getting deliciously rumpled by the wind. He's wearing sunglasses, which I regret, because I really wish I could see the look in his eyes.

I stop at the edge of the pool, unsure of what to do.

"Well, Walker?" I taunt, suddenly desperate to cover myself. "Are we swimming or are we swimming?" I don't wait for his reply; I simply leap in the pool, cannonball style.

Not very sexy.

But at least I'm no longer on display before his discerning gaze.

I'm barely surfacing when there's a splash, and I open my eyes underwater to see Kit's athletic form in a dive that brings him easily to the middle of the pool. He reaches me, his arms coming around me under water, as he pulls us both up.

I gasp as we surface, laughing. Kit slicks back my hair, a smile on his lips as we look at each other. He then dips his head in the water, slicking his hair back from his face.

His gorgeous face.

He's so close. I make out the rivulets of water on his lashes, his nose, his eyebrows. I want to kiss each one. Lick each one. Sip each one.

"Hey again," he rumbles in that British accent of his.

I smile. "Hey again," I say back. Shy. Nervous. Happy. Lusty.

On impulse, I splash some water on him. He evades it, then chuckles. "Oh, so that's how it's going to be?" He quirks an eyebrow before he attacks me like a shark, and I swim as hard as I can to keep him from catching me.

He's too fast for me. He pins me against the pool ledge, leaning his head to mine.

Our lips connect. His tongue strokes mine. I shiver, but I'm not cold.

He slants his head then kisses me harder, as if he's been waiting all day to do it.

He eases back, his voice a rasp. "I've needed to do that for hours."

"Since when…?" I have to know the answer. I crave it like air. Like I crave another kiss. Like I crave *Kit*.

He strokes a wet thumb down my wet cheek, leaning down to part my lips again. "Since I first met you, Miss Gorgeous—" *lick* "—feisty—" *lick* "—Croft."

I moan and let him kiss me for a little while longer.

We spend the evening stealing more kisses. Swimming. Resting on the loungers and holding a diving contest, where we rate each other's dives. My competitive streak comes to the surface, and I bring my best dives into play. He seems surprised that I can pull a mean dive, not just a cannonball. Take *that*, sexy Kit Walker! Ha.

Still in the pool, we sip on drinks he brings us from the outdoor bar, and talk about the app. The launch date.

During a lull in the conversation, Kit pulls me a little closer to him and starts kissing me again.

"What are we doing, Kit?" I ask, breathless.

"What do you mean?" He regards my lips as if he plans to feast on them, again.

"I mean…what are we doing? Does this have a name? We can't date. Not really, not without everyone finding out. So what are we doing?"

"We can date, Alex." He frowns in confusion, as if not liking the idea that I feel like we can't. "To bloody hell if they don't like it." He cups my face, his expression fierce. "We're grown adults. We don't have to let this interfere with business."

"It's not that easy, Kit. Plus, say we dated. Then what? What happens when we tire of it? Will you fire me when you're ready to discard me?"

"What makes you think I'd tire of you…" Kit glances away, his jaw clenched as if the thought bothers him, then he looks at me, and ducks his head to nudge my nose with his and force my gaze to his. "I want you, Alex. I want you more than bloody—" He exhales, his nostrils flaring as his intense male gaze drills into my very heart. "I really want you," he concludes, tipping my face back.

"I want you, too. I want this. I'm just…afraid."

"Don't be. Not of me. Or this." He scoops me out of the pool and sets me down on the lounger.

Our hands are wet as we touch each other. Kit expertly peels off my bikini.

"God, Alex, look at you," he rasps, stroking his hands down my body.

"Kit," I moan, arching to get closer. Too desperate

for him to wait, I sit up and start kissing him, pushing him back onto the lounger so that I can straddle him. In one motion, I push down his swim trunks and impale myself on him. Just like that.

He groans as I have my way, moving furiously over him, unable to get enough. Unable to quench this thirst, this need, this desire for him. Unable to decide whether this is the smartest decision I've ever made—or whether giving myself to this man is something I will one day come to regret.

Right now, I'm too undone by his kiss and touch to care.

Kit finally brings me up to his room. As I dry off one last time, Kit stands there with his towel wrapped around his hips, studying his phone. "We're supposed to beta this thing." He motions to the app as he stands at the foot of the bed, watching me climb in—fully naked.

I nod and reach for my phone, and open the app as Kit types something. His message stares back at me.

You look beautiful right where you are.

I look at him. He smiles, raises a brow and types more.

Like you belong there.

My throat constricts with emotion. I meet his stare head-on. "I feel beautiful. And like I could get used to this. That's what scares me," I say out loud.

He tosses his phone aside and moves forward as he whips open his towel. I don't know who moves first, but both of us are suddenly aligned, his hair in my hands, my hair in his, our bodies flat and touching everywhere. We kiss in silence, our bodies doing the talking.

Every heated whisper sears me. He tells me I feel just right. That he can't get enough of me. There's yearning in every word and caress, in every kiss, every groan of his, every moan he coaxes out of me. And in this stolen moment when nothing else exists but him, me, us, I could swear that Kit Walker is falling as hard as I am.

Nineteen

Despite my excitement and the fact that I can't seem to spend a few minutes without thinking of him, I hear nothing from Kit for the rest of the week.

I've seen him in the office, but only at meetings. No stolen touches this time.

At our next meeting with my team on Friday, I catch Kit looking at me with a frown. But he makes no move to touch me. Nor smile at me.

What's going on?

As we adjourn the meeting, Ben asks me to join him and Angela and Tim for drinks, and Kit lifts his head from the opening page design printout he asked to take.

Feeling Kit's gaze on me like a weight, I tell Ben I'm busy.

Ben seems displeased and walks out, and Kit smiles

to himself as he returns his gaze to the papers. I'm suddenly angry at him and want to punch him. Instead, I'm glad the week is over as I head home that afternoon and wonder what's going on.

Is he already done with me? I'm furious. Most of all hurt. Because there's one unerring thought in the back of my mind that won't leave me alone:

I should have seen this coming.

Monday I dress with care, wanting to look perfect. Wanting to look into Kit's eyes and find something— a clue as to what happened between us.

I know something is wrong the moment I arrive at work.

When I enter the room, I feel as if everyone is nervous around me.

I'm suddenly nervous as well, though of course *I* have cause to be nervous. I slept with the boss. Not just once, but repeatedly.

And he hasn't mentioned it for a whole week. No text. No word.

How can someone just forget to call after a night like the one we had? God, the way he touched me felt…like he was *cherishing* me. Like he craved me as much as I craved him. And the flowers that first night he invited me over—from Turkey!

Then again, I guess when you sleep with a billionaire, you never know what constitutes a big gesture. It probably was nothing for him to have those flowers delivered, barely making a dent in his bank account.

Suddenly, I feel like the romance is dying. Once

the flower fades to nothingness, so will my connection with Kit.

I need to stop thinking I know the man. I clearly know nothing at all.

There's a soft knock on my office door. I look up and spot Angela. She's not her usual self. She isn't smiling, her body language withdrawn and stiff. She's probably a mirror image of my own mood. I frown, dread pricking like a little thorn in my stomach.

"Everything okay, Angela?"

She doesn't say anything, closing the door behind her quietly. "The boss wants to see you."

"Okay…"

Angela bites her nail self-consciously.

"He seemed…pissed."

I shake my head in confusion. "Talk to me. Why is everyone on edge?"

"I don't know. Maybe because…you are? You seem on edge. Ben, too. And Kit." Angela perches herself on the chair opposite mine. "I only bumped into Kit in the elevator. He told me to fetch you. He wants you in his office immediately."

"Why do you think he was angry?"

"I don't know. He was just…unusual. Not like the calm and easygoing Kit we've all come to know and love."

My hands are shaking as I shut down my browser. "Thanks, Angela. I'll be right there."

I'm perplexed. What could possibly faze the most unfazeable man I've ever met?

Things take another turn for the worse when I head

out of my office and hear a commotion right by my door. I see Alastair walking toward me.

Dread churns in my stomach. Because something tells me his presence means nothing good.

I'm suddenly paranoid. Oh god. I can barely look him in the eye as he heads toward me, looking determined. "Alexandra. Can we talk?"

"Yes, Alastair…of course. Where should we talk… Kit wanted to see me…"

I scramble to follow as Alastair quickly strides in the direction of the elevators.

"Kit's office is fine."

I nod nervously, chewing the inside of my cheek as I follow him into the car. Once we reach the executive floor, Alastair steps out and heads to the end of the hall. He knocks on Kit's door. "Kit. We're coming in, boy."

Alastair swings the door open, and my heart does a little pitiful pitter-patter as I walk in and see Kit bent over his computer, wearing a frustrated expression on his handsome face.

He looks up, his eyes dark. Clouded. My heart sinks down to my feet.

What's going on?

Surprise replaces the dark look in Kit's eyes when he spots his father, and the tension in his face morphs into shock as his eyes widen.

"Dad?"

Kit's gaze meets mine and I see confusion there. I feel so guilty about what we did that it's an effort to take a decent breath.

"Alex," Kit's voice drops a decibel as he addresses me.

He looks all business.

The guy who held me in his arms only a week ago is gone.

"Kit, you wanted to see me," I say, after clearing my throat.

Kit glances at his father, his jaw squaring and his gaze shuttering.

"Of course. Show her," Alastair tells Kit as if answering his silent question. Alastair motions to the conference table. "I'll wait here."

Alastair pulls out a chair, while Kit waits for me to approach his desk.

"What's wrong?" I ask quietly, so that only Kit can hear.

"My father and I received this email," Kit whispers, jerking his chin to motion me even closer.

I go around his desk, trying not to inhale Kit's cologne as I peer at his computer screen. He clicks open an attachment.

I try to remain aloof and cool. When the window opens, I can't help but gasp.

The photo is dark, but the content is clear. It's an image of Kit and me out by the pool. Naked. There's no question who's in the picture—Kit's back is turned, but his garden is so recognizable that anyone working here would know it's him.

On the other hand, my face is in perfect focus. I blush. How many people have seen this? I don't particularly care that my body is exposed. It's more the fact that now everyone knows my secret. And Kit's.

"I'm so sorry. I don't know who sent it to us," Kit

murmurs to me. I notice how dark and lifeless his amber eyes look today.

I see the honest frustration there, and while a part of me wants to reach out and comfort him, I'm so hurt and shocked by the image that I can't even move.

I'm completely dumbfounded. I stare at the photo again. Then the email subject line catches my eye: *Desperate for a promotion much?*

Humiliated, I move away from the computer, feeling nauseated. I don't want to leave Cupid's Arrow. I found a home in this company. So what the hell am I meant to do when a naked photo of me with the boss is out there, circulating—emailed to both my bosses? I clutch my stomach, the shock feeling like physical pain.

And that's when it hits me.

It just hits me.

That Alastair is watching me. Alastair…whom I have completely betrayed.

Who will fire me, on the spot, like I *deserve* to be fired.

"I—I can't believe this. How did someone even get the photo?" I ask Kit as he starts heading for the conference table. I follow him, my whole body trembling.

Someone else might try to claim Photoshop was involved, but I'm not an idiot. I work on a design team. And the people who work for me would clearly see the image had not been retouched.

"Come here. Both of you," Alastair demands, rapping his knuckles on the table.

Kit's jaw is clenched, and he motions me forward. Heart sinking in dread, I force myself to meet Alastair's gaze as we reach the conference table. I can't believe anyone would do this to me.

I feel sick.

I exhale, trying to get myself under control.

Kit takes the head of the table, and I sit down to his left. Right across from Alastair. Who used to love me. Adore me. And now… I dread looking into his eyes and seeing the disappointment there.

"You're not fit to manage this company," Alastair tells Kit plainly. "And since this young lady here has been sleeping with you, she's been failing to give me an honest report about you as well…" Alastair levels me with a glance, his normally kind eyes fierce. "I expected more from you, Alex."

Kit. Moving inside me. Touching me. Kissing me.

"Alastair…" I begin.

"It's my fault. I seduced her."

Both Alastair and I whip around to stare at Kit.

"She was a pain in my ass." Kit's eyes gleam as he holds my gaze. "I wanted her off my back. I decided to seduce her and get some space to actually get some work done around here."

I can't believe what I'm hearing.

I blink. My eyes sting.

"It was all my fault," Kit repeats, addressing his father now. "Alex did nothing wrong. Her only mistake was trusting a guy like me not to take advantage of her."

"That's not true." My voice is stern, belying the way I really feel: like I'm breaking inside. "You didn't take advantage of me." I shake my head in bewilderment. "Kit…how could you say that?"

Do you really mean it?

Alastair seems thoughtful. As Kit looks at his father, waiting for Alastair's decree, I feel my cheeks turn hotter and hotter. The room starts feeling too small, claustrophobically small.

"It was all on me, Alastair," I whisper, emphatically shaking my head as I meet both their gazes. "I'll resign. I cannot taint Cupid's Arrow, nor your reputation—"

"You're not going anywhere," says Kit.

"Absolutely not," Alastair repeats. His phone starts buzzing on the table. He picks up. "Talk to me," he barks into the receiver.

I meet Kit's unreadable gaze. I'm so hurt I can't even speak for fear of crying in front of him.

As Alastair listens to the caller on the other end of the line, I search for the words I need to tell Kit.

"You're trying to take the blame," I quietly accuse, "but I won't let you."

"Watch me," he answers. Just as quietly, and with steely resolve.

Alastair hangs up.

"That was my systems security guy. I asked him to trace the email. It was surprisingly easy. Ben Roberts is the sender."

Disbelief shakes me. "Ben?" I gasp. My whole world tilts. How did he even know I would be there?

That's when it hits me. Ben was with us in the elevator when Kit told me he'd see me that night. Did he follow me?

Completely shocked by the news, I shake my head in denial. "Ben is my friend. He'd never do this to me."

Kit narrows his eyes and leans back in his chair, crossing his arms as he studies me. "You're so sure?"

"I'm sure. He's my friend!" I insist, still unwilling to let the truth sink in.

Kit's frown is deepening by the second. He tilts his head, a cloud of darkness shrouding his eyes. "Did you set me up, Alex? Arrange for him to be there? Were you two planning to oust me from the company?"

"Excuse me?"

Once Kit speaks his fears out loud, it's as if the possibility of it all hits him, and he laughs in disgust. "Wow. The one woman who's breached my defenses was out to get me all along." He pushes his chair back and stands, pacing, clenching his hands into fists at his sides.

"Kit, I would never…"

He turns around to face me, his eyes shooting daggers at me. "You kept defending him—covering up for him. He was always around you…" Kit's features grow tighter, his voice angrier with every word. Each one a slap to my pride, my heart and my wishful hopes for what could have been.

Alastair watches in silence, then looks me dead in the eye. "You never did want my son here, did you, Alex?"

"Alastair—"

"I'll accept your resignation. Have it delivered to Kit by tomorrow at the end of the day." Alastair pushes his chair back, his stance closed off and unapproachable.

I sit there, blinking, as Alastair gives Kit a warning. "I trusted you, Kit, and you've betrayed my trust. I'll move back into my office and watch things from up close. *I* will determine whether you're fit to run Cupid's Arrow. Is that clear?"

"Crystal," Kit says tightly.

Kit's gaze never leaves me as Alastair exits the office.

I have trouble forcing myself to stand.

My eyes burn in embarrassment and my heart is in tatters in my chest. I can hardly walk, but I *can't wait* to get out of here. I stand up slowly, as gracefully as I can, and start for the door when Kit's words stop me.

"Look at me."

Twenty

I freeze. Then I slowly turn and meet Kit's hurt gaze. I can barely stand the pain I see there. The need.

I bite my lip and watch him as I draw in a breath.

Breathe, Alex. Explain!

I know that there's chemistry between human beings. Not just between males and females, but between every being of our species. Some underlying connection, sensation, *instinct*.

I know that we sometimes can't help being repelled by someone we don't even know very well, but I'd never really experienced the *opposite*. Being viscerally magnetized to the point where it doesn't even matter that you don't know shit about this other person or what he's been doing his whole life. You just want to get rid of the physical distance between you; you want to get closer.

I never in my life imagined how painful it would feel to cross that distance only to be acutely aware of what you're missing the moment an abyss opens up between you—an abyss impossible to cross.

"I swear, Kit," I breathe, needing him to understand, "that I had no part in it. Do you think I really wanted to be humiliated like this? In front of your father? A man I admire and respect? In front of *you*, when all I wanted was—"

I inhale to calm down, and cut myself off from saying more. But the way Kit is looking at me, as if gazing at a stranger, is tearing me up inside.

I've never felt as bereft as I am now, when the warmth in his eyes that was there only a week ago is completely gone.

"You were against me from the start," Kit says with quiet anger, the hurt intensifying in his eyes. "You wanted me out of here. Having you in the picture would make you the least likely suspect to set me the bloody hell up," he hisses, clearly believing this complete bullshit.

"I would *never* do something this awful to anyone. Never. Much less to you, or myself! True, I didn't think you had it in you. I thought you were lazy, that you knew nothing about work because you had no experience. That you were nothing but a playboy and I guess I was right, huh? Because you played me. You played me, Kit Walker. You just told your father—"

"I was trying to shoulder the blame and get you off the hook. I didn't want you out of the picture for good, or for Alastair to fire you. Unlike *your* own plans for me," he spits out.

I gasp.

"So you were lying to your father? You're saying I did mean more to you than just a simple seduction? Really? I meant so much that you don't even have any idea of who I am or what my true feelings are!"

I make to leave, but Kit blocks my path. "I don't know about your feelings, Alex, but I bloody damn well know you were the most vocal protesting my presence here, and that you've turned my bloody head upside down. Not for one minute did I—"

"Why didn't you call?" I blurt out. Forgetting about the photo for now. Forgetting about everything but the one fact that hurts me the most. He clenches his jaw.

"I didn't want to speak over the phone… I was going to come and see you this week. But after the email…" He lets the words die off.

Die like the room full of roses that he wowed me with, and the memory of our time together.

"I know you were trying to defend me from Alastair when you said all that. But I can't help but believe that part of it could be true. That you just wanted to get control over me, in any way you knew how," I accuse, taking a deep breath. "I'm sorry I ever met you, Kit. I'm sorry I ever fell for your bullshit." I whirl around. "I'll turn in my resignation tomorrow."

Then I walk away from Kit, even though I'm completely certain I've fallen in love for the first time in my life.

Dreading that I leave with the man I love thinking I betrayed him.

Maybe I did.

I followed my heart and betrayed every single thing I believe in, for him.

Wow. What a way to learn my lesson. Now when my walls go back up, I'll be sure to let nobody in. Ever. Especially a player like Kit Walker.

The next day, I finish packing up my desk, logging on to my work computer one last time. I can see how much has changed just from the attitude in the room. No one here has said a word since I told them I was quitting. They're all shocked. They asked why. I said, with a fake smile, that I wanted to pursue other opportunities.

Bullshit. They all know it's bullshit. Especially Ellie.

But I'm so heartbroken, I don't even want to talk about it.

At a certain point, I whispered to my best friend, "Please just stop asking me why. You know it's because of Kit."

"You have feelings for him," she whispered back.

I nodded, and that was enough to make her understand.

When lunch hour hits, I quietly leave the office to find Kit.

My hands tremble at the thought of what will happen. I'm officially turning in my resignation. I'm leaving the place I love. I'll need to go out there and hustle, just because of everything that I've ruined. It would break me if I ruined Helena's future as well as mine.

I wish I could tell Kit how I really feel. I wish I had the guts to come out in the open and tell him that I love him, that I would never do anything like this to the man I love.

But he didn't go into this little affair expecting to hear *I love you* from me. So I won't say it, and hopefully one day soon, after a couple of years of not having to see him every day, this feeling will go away—even if that stupid email won't.

But the truth is, Kit Walker opened my eyes.

That night with the roses, I never thought I could feel so alive.

I never thought there could be more to life than just working.

And now it's all crumbled before me, leaving behind only an illusion of happiness that seems too out of reach for me now.

Kit's office is quiet as I stand outside.

I can remember the days when I'd walk past and hear someone inside, laughing at one of his jokes, trying to butter him up. Now, there's only silence. Has Kit changed as much as I have? Has he left his player days behind because of the nights we shared?

I don't know. That's not my business anymore.

I knock on the door before I can change my mind.

"Come in," Kit says, his voice low and muffled. When I open the door, he looks up from some papers he's reviewing and I see his beautiful face, probably for the last time. His features dissolve into surprise. I curse myself. I should have called to tell him the time when I would stop by. It would have better prepared us both for this moment.

"Hey…sorry to drop in like this. But I'm all packed and ready and wanted to give you this."

Kit is paralyzed, still holding one of the papers he was reading in his hand. He seems to be struggling to find words. "No, no, of course. Sit down, take a seat." He drops the paper as if it singes him, watching me walk cross his office.

He's cleaned it up—and noticing how professional he looks only makes my chest feel heavier.

I sit down cautiously, not sure how to proceed. I thread my fingers together, staring at my lap.

"How are you?" Kit asks, his voice deep and low, but tentative. I swallow hard to rid myself of the lump in my throat, but it doesn't help.

"Things…things aren't going that well for me. As you know. So I just want to get this over with." I take a deep breath, the weight of his stare almost unbearable. "I promised your father that I would help you settle into the company. I feel that I did my best but allowed my personal feelings to rule some of my actions…and I betrayed him. I know you think I betrayed you, too, but I want you to know that's not the case."

There's a silence.

I raise my head and when our eyes meet, there almost seems to be a crackle in the room.

We stare off for a minute, then slowly, Kit's forehead creases and he leans across the desk toward me. "I interviewed Ben yesterday. Give me one more day, Alex. Don't resign yet."

"What do you mean?"

"I don't want you to resign yet. Give me one more day."

I shake my head. "Why?"

"Give me time," he snaps, his gaze bright and vivid. "To prove to myself and my father that you're innocent."

I shake my head. What does it matter anyway? I'm not sure that I can go back to being the way it was before, when I sort of hated Kit. Or that I can go on as if nothing happened between us. I'm emotionally invested now. I shake my head because I can't say any of this to him, though I really wish that I could.

"There's nothing for me here anymore," I tell him. He leans away, looking like I just slapped him. I try to backpedal.

"I don't mean… I mean in terms of my career. I've progressed as far as I can go. Nothing will change my mind now, Kit. I have to leave after that photo. After today, I won't be coming back. I hope… I hope you can forgive me any problems I've caused."

Kit clenches his jaw tightly, dragging a hand across his face, his eyes flashing in frustration. "I do. If you're no longer happy here…then of course you have to leave. I know things have been difficult since I arrived. I know yesterday took a toll on all of us. But the company will miss you." Kit finally forces himself to meet my gaze. "I'll miss you."

My heart is somersaulting. "I'll miss you, too."

Kit swallows and I can see that he's holding back a lot of emotion. He shifts in his chair, his face forlorn. "I know you know your own mind, Alex, and if you think this is the best course of action, then it is. But I need to know. Did you turn off the notifications from the app?"

I frown in confusion.

"The beta app. Remember I told you we'd beta? I've been sending messages."

"Oh." I hang my head. "I'll admit, I never turned them on when I downloaded it."

Kit nods, taking a deep breath. "I'll let you go. So long as you promise me you'll check your inbox."

I don't understand why he's so desperate for me to read over some beta testing messages, but if those are his terms, I have to take them.

I nod, rising from my seat and holding out my hand for him to shake. He stands, too, taking it. His touch is gentle, and his fingertips brush my wrist. I try not to shiver, but it stirs something in me. I press my lips together and try not to cry. Kit doesn't let go, his eyes on mine.

"It's been a pleasure working with you."

I guess we've said everything that needs to be said between us.

I nod, my throat raw, letting his hand drop from my grip. "It's been a pleasure working with you, too."

Twenty-One

That evening, I can't help but miss my sister more than ever. I dropped off calling or messaging since my affair with Kit started. I shoot her a quick text.

Hope you're well. Miss you

She responds pretty quickly. I'm ok. Studying. Miss you too. Up for me calling?

Yes!

When she calls, I can't help but chide her in a loving manner. "Why are you calling me? You should be out having fun, not staying home doing homework."

She scoffs and I settle down on my bed, smiling for

the first time in what feels like a while. "Excuse me? Alex, *you're* the one who's told me that hard work pays off and once I'm where I want to be, I can do anything I like."

"True. Except lately I've been realizing…there's more to life than just work."

"Like what?"

I shrug. "Well, you, for example. We should talk more."

"We're in touch all the time. What's gotten into you? Where's my sister and what have you done to her?"

I smile fondly.

"Are things not good at work, Alex?"

I groan and flip to my side, pushing my cheek into my pillow while I hold my phone to my other ear. I dread telling her that I resigned. But if I can't talk to my sister, then who can I talk to? "Not really. Something happened at the office recently. It was humiliating and it was all my fault. I did something I never in a million years thought I'd do."

"What?"

I hesitate for just a moment. But Helena is twenty-one. I know she's old enough to talk to, and we've always really only relied on each other. "I slept with my boss."

"With Alastair?"

I sit up in bed from the shock and burst out laughing. "Silly! *No!* He passed the baton to his youngest son and Kit Walker is just… He surprised me. Swept me off my feet. Wormed his way into my heart. But one of my office friends leaked a photo of us… Helena, it was awful. Kit thinks I was in on it just to oust him from the company."

"Why would you oust him?"

"Well I was a bit critical when he first took over, thinking he didn't have it in him to run the company."

"Oh, Alex." She groans.

I try to recover, struggling to shake him off. "It's over now. No point rubbing salt in the wound."

"You didn't sleep with your boss—you fell in love with him. That's two totally different things."

"You're right. I did both and I don't know which is worse."

"For you? Both are bad. But both of them *together*…" She whistles dramatically. "What can I do to cheer you up?"

"Nothing. Hearing your voice helps. And maybe if you went out and had some fun, I'd know that my sister was out there being happy, and *I'd* be happy."

"Nah. It doesn't count. It needs to be you. You can't just be happy if others are. You need to make your own happiness, Alex."

"I can't. I ruined this with Kit. Though to be honest… I think he was only playing with me. And I fell for it. For all of it." My voice cracks. "I resigned, Helena."

There's a shocked gasp.

"Don't worry!" I immediately say, trying to appease her. "I'll still help you out with college and your expenses. I'm going to line up interviews—"

"Alex, that's okay. If we can pay for college that's great but if not, I'll be okay. I don't want you bearing my burden."

"You're never a burden. It's you and me against the world. Right?" I tease.

But that should also include…you know. Having lots of friends so that it doesn't hurt you if one betrays you, and having lots of fun so that if one day you lose your job, you don't feel this giant emptiness.

"Yes." Though she doesn't sound as playful as she did only moments ago. "Alex, you'll find something," Helena promises. "You're a genius at what you do and any company would be lucky to have you. Any guy, too."

"Kit doesn't believe that," I whisper. "Falling for him really hurts because even after all this, I want more and I'm afraid…"

"Of what?"

I see Kit's amber eyes in my mind.

"Are you afraid he'll want more, too? Or that he won't and you'll be so vulnerable that he'll have the power to hurt you?"

"That. The latter," I say quietly, my chest loosening a bit when I admit that. "If you'd seen the hurt in his eyes when he thought I was conspiring with Ben, Helena."

"Maybe that's a good thing. Maybe that means he does care. Despite not wanting to. Like you."

I sigh, not wanting to believe it could be true. Not knowing what I want.

"Okay so I lack experience in the romance department," Helena continues, "but if I'd just resigned and gotten my heart broken, I'd tell you what my ballsy big sister would say."

"What would she say?" I play along.

"That the only way to conquer my fears is through action. And that fear leads the way to the greatest opportunities."

I smile. "I'm glad I've made the effort to put you through Stanford. You're so wise."

"Shush!" She laughs again, and it's such a lovely sound that part of me wants to trap that joy in a jar and save it for her forever. So that she never forgets how joy feels, never forgets to laugh like that. "But I'm glad, too. I love you," she says. "Alex…thank you for all your efforts. I never want you to think that I take them for granted. One day I'm going to pay you back in full."

"Seeing you succeed in doing something you love is enough for me, Helena. Please don't worry. I'll keep you posted on how the interviews go. And I love you, too."

I smile as I hang up, the warmth of my sister's voice lingering as I lie in bed, wondering what I regret the most. Losing my job? Or opening my heart and letting someone in?

Opening my heart and letting *Kit Walker* in?

It's been a week since I resigned. A week of not being able to wake up without feeling as if my whole world just came crashing down on me. Work used to be everything to me. Now I'm cooped up in my apartment, lonely and depressed. I miss Helena more than ever. I worry about getting a new job—after the way things went down at Cupid's Arrow. I've been searching online, but don't feel like I can walk into an interview without breaking down in tears yet.

I wish I could hug Helena, who loves me no matter how badly I've made a mess of things.

I even miss my parents and wish that we were closer, that they would occasionally check in and not be so busy all the time whenever I call.

And I miss Kit.

All in all, I think it's fair to say that my life is broken in every way that counts.

My co-workers were sad to see me go. Some of them cried. Ellie cried. She's stayed in touch this week, telling me that the office isn't the same without me. That they're looking for a replacement but that the whole team doesn't want anyone else. She's asking me why I resigned. They all feel betrayed—as if I left them. She also mentions that Ben was out on some sort of leave right after I resigned, but then he came back.

I can't believe how much trouble a fling with my boss has caused me. I've heard Angela talk about her many sexual endeavors before, and never once has one of them landed her in so much crap. But now I realize how wrong I was to think that I could get away with it. This whole disaster was never going to be smooth sailing.

That'll teach me, I suppose.

It's Saturday morning. I'm lounging in front of the TV, trying to think of ways to pass the weekend quickly all alone. Even with the TV on, my ears are sensitive to how quiet it is. It's putting me on edge.

I flit between activities. I try reading. I watch more TV. I take a bubble bath, but it's not relaxing. Something feels off, though I can't put my finger on what it is.

The afternoon drags on and on. I grow restless and

anxious. I can't stop thinking about Kit, while at the same time, I can't bear to remember the hurt in his eyes when he thought I was in cahoots with Ben.

Ben. Gosh I hope somebody punches him.

Though I can't blame him for everything. Because it was *me* in that picture, and I can't pretend otherwise.

I'm nauseated, having become one of those women I've always pitied who sleep with their bosses.

Suddenly remembering what Kit asked me about our messages on the app, I pull out my phone and hesitate. Do I want to read them? Then I remember our work on the design and on impulse, I open up the app, eyeing it and realizing that the new design is up.

It's so gorgeous.

Incredible.

Edgy.

Modern.

My heart soars for a moment.

I log in to my inbox, curious now.

And there *is* a message. At least a dozen messages, actually. From Kit.

Twenty-Two

I sift through the list, wondering what it is that Kit wants me to check out. I was wrong. There must be around twenty of them, all clumped together, one after the other. They don't look like they're work related. They look personal.

I open the first.

Alex, I just want you to know that I really enjoyed the past two nights. I hope you had as much fun as I did.

I close the message. Did he write this after we downloaded the app and had that amazing weekend together? My heart squeezes as I head to the next one.

Are you doing anything tonight? I would love to take you out for dinner again.

A lump rises in my throat. I wonder how long ago he sent this one. I check the date and realize it was Wednesday. Right after he asked me to his place and we went swimming. So he wasn't avoiding me after that night—he was just messaging me and not getting an answer. I'm feeling nauseated as I look at the next note.

You just left the office. I don't know what to think about things. If you weren't in it with Ben…then I'm the biggest asshole I've ever met. This is killing me.

My phone trembles in my hand as I open the next. This one is longer. More detailed than the others.

Ben admitted he acted alone. He wanted to hurt you and me both. Your resignation letter sits on my desk, and I want to rip it in two. I want you back. I want you back with me.

Please see me tonight, I'll meet you anywhere, just let me tell you this in person.

I shift through the remaining messages, tears streaming down my cheeks. This isn't what I expected at all. Each note holds a piece of Kit's heart, and each one I read breaks mine a little more.

I wipe desperately at my eyes. I promised to read them all, so that's what I have to do.

The final note is from today.

You promised you'd read your messages. Are you reading this at all? I'm out on the ledge here, Alex. At least meet with me so I can tell you in person what this means to me. What you mean to me.

My hand lingers on the screen, but I don't have the courage to reply. My heart has just grown wings, but I'm too scared to reach out. Too scared to hope that Kit means it.

Ellie comes over and gets me out of the house later that afternoon. We decide to head downtown.

"So are you really going through with the interviews?" she asks as we stand in front of a clothing store window on Miracle Mile.

"I have to. I can't leave Helena hanging and I need to go on with my life. I'm just hoping Kit gives me a good reference." I remember the notes on the app, and emotion rises in my throat again.

"He's completely bereft, you know," Ellie says, as if reading my mind.

I raise my eyes to hers.

"Kit," she clarifies. "Are you really not coming back? It seems to me that he didn't want you to go."

"It was too messy, Ellie. There was a photo of… Kit and me. It was sent to Alastair and Kit. Kit thought I was in on it to oust him from the company. I couldn't bear the look of betrayal in his eyes. Worse, Alastair… well, I betrayed him for real."

"He and Kit are tense at the office. I don't think either of them is happy to see you gone. But why didn't you tell me about this before?"

"It was hard to talk about it. Especially when it was Ben who sent it."

"Ben! Oh my gosh, that snake!" she cries. "No wonder he got fired yesterday! He was called into Kit's office and Angela says when he came out he was white as a sheet. He packed up his things and security escorted him out."

"I can only imagine how that went."

"He was in Kit's office for a long while," she says with an evil little giggle.

Was that when Kit drilled him on whether or not he acted alone? And why does it matter? He believed the worst of me. He never called. He told his father he'd just played me.

But you know that the reality is actually in the messages he sent you, saved in the Cupid's Arrow app, another part of me whispers.

Shaking that thought aside, I exhale and continue walking down Miracle Mile, window shopping and inhaling the breeze—when a familiar SUV pulling into a parking space about a block away snags my attention.

It's a white Range Rover. The one I saw when I went to Kit's house.

My heart trips as I spot the figure stepping out of it.

"Holy…" Ellie trails off as we both watch Kit approach.

My heart starts drumming.

My palms start sweating.

Every blood vessel in my body constricts with yearning.

I want to run to him and kiss him. I want to punch

his chest for hurting me and then kiss him. I want to do a whole lot of things. But all I do is stare at him as he stops before me, a small smile on his lips.

"Ellie," he says.

"Kit."

Even when he greets Ellie, his amber gaze is solely on me. Eyes I'd never thought I'd see again. And they are so warm. So hot as they look at me. It's as if my blood is boiling from the heat.

"Alex," Kit finally murmurs, his tone a decibel lower than usual.

I only nod briskly. "We're out window shopping. Looking for new suits for my upcoming interviews. I hope you're well, Kit. It's nice to see you." I hurriedly brush past but he catches my elbow to halt me.

"Alex, don't go."

I freeze. His grip is warm and gentle on my elbow. I look down at his hand. I'm aching in places so deep, they'll never see the light. *He* was the light that touched them, set them on fire. Without him it's dark and lonely. My whole life is dark and lonely.

"I can't do this," I whisper.

"Alex, look at me."

Inhaling, I raise my gaze up to his throat. His lips. His perfect nose. And look into his eyes.

"Did you get my messages?" There's hope in his words, in his voice.

"Yes," I manage to say, emotion overcoming me as I pry free of his hold.

"And?"

He drops his hand, waiting impatiently for my answer.

"And it's too late." I turn away but Kit says something else.

"I love you, Miss Croft."

I halt on the spot, the words resonating in my mind, my chest, my heart. I almost laugh when he calls me Miss Croft, like I demanded he call me the first day we met.

"Or would you rather I call you Alexandra?"

I turn, and a wicked smile curves the corners of his lips.

"Alexandra Croft… I love you. Despite wanting to keep things professional. Despite thinking maybe you'd betrayed me. Despite feeling scared out of my bloody wits because what I felt for you was too strong. I still loved you. I was wrong, and I cannot tell you how sorry I am. I was afraid you'd gotten too firm a hold of me. And you know what, Alexandra?"

My legs are trembling as he takes a step closer.

"I was right to be concerned." His expression fierce and meaningful, he starts to nod. "Because nobody has ever gotten this firm a hold of me before. I've never thought of anyone as much as I think of you. Or wanted, or respected, or admired, or needed a woman as much as I need you."

His words have broken through my barriers and I can't pretend that I don't feel the same about him.

Kit stands there, wearing nothing but a pair of gray jogging pants and a white T-shirt, his expression raw and open. It's like he doesn't care who hears. Ellie. Whoever passes by. It's like he just needs to get this off his chest. And I know how he feels.

Because I have so much to say to him, too.

I want to believe him.

I want to leap into his arms.

A party boy at the best of times, Kit has kept a cool demeanor from the start, unfazed by most people and situations. But now I've realized that just as he's had an impact on me, I've thrown him off his usual ways, too.

Even before we met, he had all that potential to do well but wasn't driven, was more interested in socializing than climbing a career ladder. But now I see a totally hot businessman before me, one who can get serious when he needs to and have fun when he wants, and I wonder why I saw so many faults in him in the beginning. When maybe I'm the one who's a bit of an extremist, who thinks the only respectable thing to do in life is work, putting aside almost everything else.

Neither of us was entirely wrong. But neither of us was right, either. Having both things in your life can make you happy. And having someone you love to share them with?

Our gazes hold, and a tear slips down my cheek.

"I'll give you two a moment," Ellie mutters.

I think we both totally forgot she was still there.

We nod, but never take our eyes away from each other.

Kit's gaze glimmers with heat and possessiveness as he looks at me. I'm basically panting in the middle of the street, breathless from fear of what I'm about to say.

"You hurt me," I whisper.

"You hurt me, too," he murmurs back.

"I'm not only talking about the email. You pulled away from me, and it hurt me."

"I was coming to terms with the fact that I have feelings for you, Alex," he says, with an apologetic nod. "Can you give a guy a moment to get his bearings after you knock him off his damn bloody feet here?"

I laugh softly, my eyes still stinging. "Maybe. But you caused some chaos in my life, Kit. Quite a lot."

"I know, and I'll do anything necessary to make it up to you."

Silence falls after his promise.

I can't stop trembling.

"I love you, Alex," he says again, watching me as he takes one last step forward, so that our bodies almost touch. "Please believe me when I say I never wanted to hurt you. That whole Ben thing threw me for a loop. He was always hanging around you, and it made me jealous. The mere idea of you and him being together while all I wanted was to make you mine drove me crazy." He shakes his head. "I drilled him. For hours. He wouldn't admit his guilt. When he finally did, he confessed to acting alone. He doesn't want us together, Alex. He wants you, and I can't blame him for that. But he can't have you…"

A light appears in Kit's eyes as he tips my chin up, holding my gaze with his.

"He can't have you, because you gave me everything you had…and I'm keeping you. I'm dating you. I'm protecting you. I'm…into you, Miss Croft."

Another tear slips, this one a happy one.

After everything we've been through, I can't believe

this is me. That Kit Walker, this gorgeous, British hunk, stands before me, opening up.

I love him, too.

I want to throw myself into his arms and plead that he never leave me. I want to kiss him. To ask him to show me everything he wrote to me in those notes with his voice, his touch. His actions. In a grand gesture, like those black roses.

I reach up to stroke a fingertip across Kit's lower lip. He smiles at that, as though approving of my move. *You like that, Mr. Walker? Well, here goes nothing.* I take a deep breath.

"Those messages you sent to me... I didn't want to reach out because I was afraid they weren't true. I was hurting too much over you. I was sad that you'd doubt me...but you're right. In the beginning I didn't want you. I misjudged you. But after getting to know you... Kit, I've fallen and there's no going back—and neither would I want to go back. Not to a life without you."

Kit smothers my cheeks in his big hands. He kisses me so fiercely that I think he'll never let go. I seize his hard jaw and kiss him back. I've never kissed a guy so wildly before. I close my eyes, tears spilling as I realize I haven't messed this up. It's going to be okay. We can make this work.

Ellie walks Kit and me over to his Range Rover, telling me to give her a call later. Then she heads home.

As he drives us to his place, Kit takes my hand across the console.

"We need to tell Alastair. Tell him that we'd like to

work together again. That we want another shot. If he forgives me for betraying his trust, he might consider taking me back—"

"He knows you weren't conspiring with Ben. And what we did wasn't reckless. We kept it strictly professional in the office. And it wasn't wrong, Alex. He'll want you back. *I* want you back. At the office and in my life." Kit looks at me, his gorgeous face tight with resolve. "Don't fret, Alex." He shakes his head, a smile on his lips. "We'll try to make him see."

Biting my lip, I nod.

When we arrive, Kit comes around the car to help me out. After he ushers me inside, and closes the door, I take his hand and lead him through his lavish house toward the living room.

I sit him down, prepping myself for the craziest, most intense sex of my life.

"Alex, you're scaring me a bit…"

I chuckle without much humor. "No, it's just that… I want to eat you up with kisses."

His eyebrows shoot up in amusement. "I wouldn't object to that."

His arm snakes out and goes around my waist, drawing me down on his lap.

Silence ensues. I glance up at him, wanting to know what his face will reveal. His features are in anarchy, his eyes bright with lust and tenderness. "Bloody woman, you're driving me crazy. Come here. I've missed you. How can I miss someone I met only this year so damn much?"

"I've wondered the same thing," I reply, stroking my fingertip along his lips.

I hold my breath, wondering what he'll say next.

Then, to my surprise, he laughs. I blink in shock, watching his entire face light up. He squeezes me to him, nuzzling my face with his.

"Shit, are you really here?" he whispers.

I furrow my brow, laughing over his excitement. "Yes, I'm here. Were you expecting someone else?"

"No, no one else." Kit pulls me into a hard hug, rocking me against him. "God, I missed you."

I can feel hot tears forming in my eyes. I thought this euphoria I'm experiencing had abandoned me for good, that I'd never again know what it's like to be truly happy. I lean in slowly and plant a gentle kiss on Kit's lips. It's salty from my tears, but I don't care. This is our moment. Nothing could ruin this right now. Nothing at all.

"Kit…"

His nose nudges mine. "Yes?"

"Let's try not to ruin this."

Kit laughs, grabbing me by my knees and pulling them open so that I'm straddling him. We snuggle up close, planting tiny kisses all over each other. For a moment, I forget all the history that led to this. Our path was rough and scary and frustrating, but knowing that it led to this moment, I wouldn't change a single part of it.

So when Kit takes my face in his big hands and starts kissing me for real, I can do nothing but open my mouth and kiss him back.

I hadn't realized how much I missed his taste until now.

He groans and eases back to look at me.

"Yes," I breathe to the unspoken question in his eyes. He wants to know that it's okay for us to be together now, without having to go to Alastair first. He wants to know if I'm really into this. I can see the relief flood his eyes at my words.

"Come here then." He smiles and stands, then bends down and scoops me up again.

"I can walk."

"I know you can walk, Miss Croft. I know you can talk, too. But right now you're doing neither."

He brings me to his bed and lowers me down on it.

He loves me. I love him.

He wants me. I want him.

And for once in my life, I have no more fear. No more restraint.

Kit comes down with me and pulls me up against him, a promise of what's to come. I like the way he takes control of the situation. Takes control of me. He captures my lips with his, and I'm lost.

His fingers move to the deep V of my shirt, where my breasts strain for release against the confines of my lacy black bra. Then he moves away again, teasing me. "Where do you want me to touch you?"

"Everywhere," I say, the words floating out on a cloud of frustration.

He chuckles at my expense. "So eager."

I grin slyly and nod. "Touch me again."

"Where?"

As if reading my thoughts, Kit bends down to run his lips along my jawline. His hand searches my calf, moving over my thigh, the sound of his caress on the fabric of my jeans roaring in my ears.

His mouth searches for mine and kisses me, his tongue stroking and taking. The sound he makes is more like a growl than a groan. All it does is heighten my own excitement.

I become lost in the moment, in the rioting sensations swirling in my body.

"Alex?"

I moan, relishing the sound of my name falling from his lips, twisting around my heart and squeezing. The way it makes me remember the day we first met. The way I suddenly realized I wanted a man for the first time in I can't remember how long.

He scoops me closer to him and lets my head fall back on the pillow, maneuvering himself so that he's not crushing me.

He's deliciously hard against my thighs, and I can't stop myself from wiggling a little, tempting him. "I'm so ready for you."

I lift myself up only long enough to shimmy out of my jeans. Kit stands and rips off his shirt, then sends his belt clattering to the floor. His boxers follow.

I pull off my top, then ease back onto the bed, wearing only my bra and panties.

"Gorgeous," Kit says, looking down at me.

He leans forward and kisses me again. The kiss to end all kisses. He plucks open my bra, easing it off my arms, then tugs down my panties until we're flesh to flesh.

I'm out of control, mindless with passion.

I rock my hips against his hand, angling for what I want, what I know he can deliver. A jolt of electricity rips through me when he strokes between my legs. But he refuses to give me what I'm aiming for, teasing me, torturing me. I begin to beg him, to plead, but he shakes his head.

"I'm going to make this last, Alex. I've been looking forward to you again for too long."

Every single cell of my body sings. "Me, too."

His hungry gaze intensifies. The strength of his desire and love for me shining there almost sends me back over the edge.

My eyes flutter closed as Kit starts to kiss me again, starting at my lips and taking a path downward.

"I want to taste you."

"Kit," I groan, tiny flecks of bright light floating in front of my eyes as he kisses beneath my belly button.

He blows out a blazing hot breath and it whispers against my belly. Then, my inner thigh as he parts my legs.

The first flick of his tongue makes my hips buck. A strangled moan escapes my mouth. It's intense and all I can do is let my head roll back into the pillow and thrust my hips forward, seeking more.

He licks at me gently, and then with greater force as he traces my entry. His thumbs push into my thighs as he holds me wide open to his lips, tongue and eyes.

"You're so beautiful, Alex," he says, grit in his tone.

Once I summon the courage to glance down at his dark head between my thighs, his gaze connects with mine. He's flushed, wild-eyed and full of passion.

His kisses are so sweet against me, his finger stroking me. Then his fingertip suddenly presses against my clit and I feel like a tree that's been struck by lightning—the bolt of burning lust rips through my entire body, setting my skin on fire.

Kit watches me as he eases back. His tongue darts out against his lips. "You taste incredible."

I want to give him something in return, but I can't manage to find the words. How do you trust your voice when your body is screaming at you to shut up and come?

One finger, then another slips inside me. He moves them in and out, never breaking eye contact with me. "What do you want me to do next?" he coaxes.

Is he really going to make me say it? "I…"

"What?"

"I want you inside me."

"Not yet."

He lowers his head and his lips cover my clit, sucking me into his hot mouth, flicking me with his tongue. His fingers never stop their forward motion, sending me hurtling toward that brick wall of pleasure again.

"Do you want me hard and deep, Alex?" he mumbles against me, sucking me again before taking one long, leisurely taste of me.

"Hurry. Please."

"I love it when you beg."

Quickly, he reaches into his slacks on the floor, pulls out his wallet and removes a condom from it.

I almost tell him not to.

"Is this what you want?" he whispers after he rolls on the condom.

"Yes!" I reach for him, pulling him closer to me, egging him on. "Please, yes."

He kisses me again, and then I feel him push inside me in one powerful thrust. God, he feels so good.

His hips move faster, increasing the urgency of our mating.

"You're so damn right and tight. So slick. I've never felt anything like this in my life."

His strangled words barely register. I cry out as I soar, digging my fingernails into his back.

He winds my hair in his fist as he pumps in and out of me, his body declaring just how much he wants me. How much he loves me.

"Kit…" My head falls back into the pillow again and I can't manage to say anything more than his name.

"Come for me, Alex. Right now."

His pace accelerates, our bodies in perfect tune. My hands are on his sinewy forearms and Kit tilts me so that my swollen clit hits his erection with every stroke.

My body fills with him. I scream his name, holding him so hard the muscles in my arms burn.

After that, we lie in each other's arms.

I'm so alive, I'm buzzing all over.

"I love you, Alexandra Croft," he murmurs in my ear. He speaks my name in a teasing tone and nudges my nose with his so that I face him.

I look up into the amber eyes of the man I love and say the words again, from the very bottom of my heart. Words I'd never said before to any man. "I love you, Kit Walker."

Twenty-Three

"Are you sure it's okay just to stop by his house? On a Sunday?"

"I'm certain. I've called already to let him know we're heading over."

I exhale nervously as Kit drives us to Alastair's place the next evening. I can't help but pray this all goes well. I've been thinking a lot about work and decided maybe I could open my own design business. I wouldn't necessarily mind it if I didn't return to Cupid's Arrow. But all of a sudden, no matter what happens with work, I desperately need Alastair to be okay with me and Kit.

Kit reaches across to seize my hand in his. "Hey. It's all right. Yeah?"

I give him a brave smile and try to fight my nerves. "Yeah."

Kit's expression warms a little more. "We'll get through this," he assures me.

"I know. I've never been surer about anything in my life than I am about me and you."

I laugh a little when I realize what I just said.

Kit looks surprised. His gaze is suddenly gleaming with something fierce and molten.

I speak hesitantly. "Is that a good thing, or bad?"

When Kit finally answers me, his tone is very intimate. "A good thing. A very good thing." His smile is slow and seductive as he lifts his hand to stroke the pad of his thumb across my chin. "I'm so in love with you, Ms. Croft. I've never been surer, either."

When we arrive at Alastair's penthouse, I'm suddenly full of instructions for Kit. "Let me do the talking first. I owe your father an explanation for the mess I made of things. And don't grab my hand or anything. I'd rather he not see me blushing. You have an amazing capacity for making me blush and I want to look professional here."

"Relax, Alex." Kit glances up at the elevator numbers as we arrive at Alastair's floor.

I'm grateful for the fact that he listened to my request to not take my hand, but he surprises me by putting his hand on the small of my back as he leads me into Alastair's beautiful apartment.

As Kit leads me down the marble halls, his light touch feels both protective and possessive. I like it. *I could get used to this very quickly.*

My heart stops for a second when we spot Alastair at the living room bar, standing next to a tall, dark-haired man. Alastair raises a wineglass he was lifting to his lips suddenly higher in the air as he greets us. "Kit. Ah! Alexandra." He sets his glass aside as he strides over.

The stranger turns and I glance into a face that's as stunningly handsome as Kit's, just a little older and more rugged. Blue eyes instead of amber.

"William," Kit greets him.

"Brother," the man says with a slow smile.

They exchange slaps on the back, then Kit introduces me. "Will, this is Alexandra Croft."

"I've heard a lot about you," William says.

In contrast to Kit, whose accent is strongly British, his brother sounds American—like his mother, I suppose.

Dreading that what William has heard may not all be good, I simply smile. "I hope you don't believe all of it," I whisper teasingly.

When he smiles back, handsome in a polished sort of way, I wonder if the family's good genes will also spread to Kit's and my babies. The thought makes me blush because I don't remember a day recently when I ever had time to even ponder whether or not I wanted babies in the future. Now I know that with the man standing next to me, I might. Who am I kidding? There's no *might* about it. I do. Soon.

After Kit and I greet Alastair with respectful embraces, the four of us settle down in the posh living room, Kit and I taking one of the two identical tan suede couches, while Alastair takes the other and William sits on a coffee-colored wingback chair. I decide to get right to the point before my nervousness starts getting the best of me. "Alastair, I want to say how sorry I am for everything that happened. I'm so ashamed of myself. I betrayed your trust, and that will never be okay. You asked me to report on Kit," I continue.

"Teach me the ropes," Kit interrupts. "And you did that well."

His brother smiles and leans back in his seat, clearly amused.

I shoot Kit a *don't help me* look, while Kit shoots me back a *you're doing great* look. I turn back to Alastair. "Yes, well… I just didn't expect to end up meeting a man I admire so much and that I could possibly…um…" Suddenly out of words, I glance at Kit for help.

He looks the opposite of nervous. It's almost as if he's glad to finally be discussing this out in the open. He gives me a teasing glance I can read only too well: *Didn't you want to do all the talking?* I start blushing when he turns his attention to his father.

"I'm in love with Alex." Kit stares Alastair dead in the eye and then gives his brother the same treatment. "I've asked her to give me a shot, give us a shot. And she's willing." His eyes are two pools of gold warmth when they slide back to me.

I let out a ragged breath, feeling red-cheeked as I laugh. "Yes. Um. That."

After a tense silence, Kit's obviously "perfect" brother releases a rumbling laugh. He shakes his head in disbelief. "Wow, brother. You really mixed business with pleasure there, didn't you."

"Yeah. Well. Neither of us planned this. But once it was staring us right in the face, we weren't willing to walk away. Not from this." Reaching out, Kit gently grasps my hand in his. My whole body warms up and the nervousness inside me eases.

"She's got it in her head to leave Cupid's Arrow for good," Kit explains to his father and brother, eyeing me for a moment with warmth in his eyes. "I'll allow it if that's what she really wants. But I know it isn't. I know this company is hers as much as it's ours. And I want her by my side. I know that with your blessing, she'll reconsider." He turns back to Alastair.

Alastair eyes us both in silence for the longest moment, then slowly shakes his head. "You two are young and have a lot to learn. Corporations are run by teams that work well together. *Trust* is integral to the process. I know you're both young… I was young once. I understand. I'm glad things have turned out well between you two—but they could have gone very differently. And I hope you both are aware of that."

"Yes," I whisper.

"That Ben guy…he's been taken care of. You did well handling that issue, Kit. And you did a good job making it so that the photo will never be seen by anyone else. But the fact of the matter is things could have really blown up in your face. It wouldn't have been good for Cupid's Arrow."

"I know, Alastair. I'm so sorry for all the trouble we caused. We should have been more careful," I say.

Alastair nods slowly. "You should have."

He sets his glass aside and leans forward, eyeing his youngest son now.

"Kit, what I'm seeing on the business front is good.

The ideas and changes that you have come up with are fresh and modern—and I'm pleased by that. I won't get in your way, in the future. I give you full leave as CEO of Cupid's Arrow." He turns to me. "Alex, you've been a great help to me. My secret weapon, for all these years. Smart, dedicated. I have watched you learn from me and grow, and I couldn't care more for you if you were my own daughter…" he trails off, and looks at both of us, his eyes jumping from one to the other as his voice becomes stern.

"But know, both of you, that if you really plan to do this, there should still be rules in place if you're to be partners in life, as well as work together at Cupid's Arrow. You have to keep your work and private lives separate. Work stays at the office when work hours finish, and your private lives stay at home. I'm sure you'll both agree it's for the good of the company, as well as your private life." A slight curve touches his lips, and he finally begins to smile.

"Agreed," Kit says quietly.

I'm speechless and so relieved, I want to cry from the gratitude I feel for being given another chance. Humbled for having screwed up so big, but being understood and accepted enough, that I can be forgiven.

Alastair comes to his feet with a big exhale, and both Kit and I stand up, too. Alastair hugs us to his sides.

My parents weren't big on hugs, but something about this makes me feel forgiveness, understanding, caring… something about this hug makes me feel a part of this family already. As we ease back, I force myself to tell

Alastair one more time how much I appreciate him. "I hope you know that I will be forever grateful to you."

He shakes his head. "The feeling is mutual, Alex. You always went above and beyond for me and Cupid's Arrow. Truthfully, I never allowed myself to dream that you and Kit could..." His eyes warm. "But know that I couldn't be happier with his choice of woman." He cups my shoulders with an encouraging squeeze, leaning in to whisper the rest. "By the looks of things, he's quite into you, young lady."

I laugh, speaking louder so that Kit can hear me. "I sure hope so. I've never felt this way before and it's quite jarring."

"Can't say I look forward to joining the club anytime soon," William remarks as he lifts his wineglass. If what Kit said about him being a control freak is true, he wouldn't like experiencing the chaotic effects of falling in love.

"To you and Alex, brother." Will looks fondly at Kit. "And your mutual success in life, love and Cupid's Arrow."

As William speaks, Kit pours us both a glass of wine and brings mine over. We join Alastair and William in a toast.

"Cheers!"

We clink glasses, and as Kit meets my gaze above the rims of our glasses, I can't help but be excited for what's in store. I want to share it all with Kit Walker. He reaches out with his free hand, squeezing my fingers in his as we drink to the future. A future that has never appealed to me more.

Epilogue

Twelve months sleeping every night in his arms, and I still haven't gotten used to the feeling of waking up in a four-poster bed next to Kit Walker.

I sigh happily and shift from my back to my side.

Kit is still asleep, his dark hair falling lazily on his forehead.

It's Sunday morning, but the sun hasn't risen yet.

I barely see the rim peeking over the horizon. Even though it's early, I've always been a morning person. And Sunday mornings always have a feeling of peace and relaxation that I love. Except now, it's even better because I have someone to share it with.

I turn to snuggle closer into Kit and I feel him stir awake. He kisses me sleepily.

"Good morning, Miss Croft."

I roll my eyes at his old joke. It takes me back to our first days at Cupid's Arrow…and our current days when he teases me at work, *still*.

"Good morning."

"You smell good," he murmurs, kissing my neck gently. "Shall I make you some breakfast?"

"I wouldn't say no to some pancakes."

Kit pecks my lips. "Pancakes it is."

"Sounds perfect." I admire Kit as he walks to the kitchen, his perky bum pushing against his black silk pajama bottoms.

I've grown so much these past few months. We both have. As a couple. Growing closer, more in love, and more attuned to each other by the day. I know better than to doubt him now, though. I've watched my player boss transform into a loving, conscientious man. The kind of man who gets out of bed on a Sunday to cook his woman a nice breakfast. I smile to myself. He's everything I could ever need and more.

I turn to get my phone from the bedside table next to me, looking for any updates on Cupid's Arrow, Helena or Alastair. It's already been a couple minutes and Kit usually asks me to come sit on the countertop with him while he cooks. Weird…

Just as I'm about to go look for him, I get a ping on my phone. It's from the Cupid's Arrow app.

Come get breakfast, Miss Croft.

I smile in confusion and get my robe on before heading to the kitchen. And right outside the bedroom door

I see a beautiful black rose. Surprise skids through me. There's a note attached to it. I open the note and it says *Follow the petals to find the next rose.*

What is this man up to? I start to feel nervous flutters in my stomach. I follow the trail of petals until it leads me to the living room. I see another black rose on top of a beautiful dress. It's such a pale pink, it's almost nude, and the material has a slight shimmer to it. I notice the path of petals keeps extending past the living room. I quickly look at the note on the stem.

Put this on. And don't forget the shoes.

I turn and sure enough, there are matching ballet flats next to it. I feel like a schoolgirl trying on her prom dress. I take it with me into the guest bathroom and quickly change. It's stunning on me. The layers of soft, shimmery, semisheer material cover my entire body. It's tight around my top and waist, and looser on the bottom, coming down to float around my calves. I slip on the flats and take a little time to brush my hair and get ready before I follow the path of petals again. It leads me to the kitchen. It's empty. I see another black rose on the countertop. Next to a brand-new, state-of-the-art Nikon camera.

Bring this with you. We might want some snapshots of this.

I'm completely at a loss now. Why do I need a camera? I notice the trail of petals continuing outside, to the patio and the pool.

I step outside, and I see the pool is covered completely in black and white petals. It looks breathtaking.

On one of the pool loungers, a single black rose rests against the cushion.

As I approach it curiously, I notice that this black rose is next to what seems to be a small golden arrow. The note simply says, *I've been hit.*

I laugh out loud now, at the cuteness of this man.

I keep following the petals, which take me past the pool, toward the gardens of his mansion. And I finally see him.

The garden has been completely transformed. There is a mirrored path leading up to a gazebo, which is completely covered in flowers of all kinds. He's standing beneath it, under hundreds of black roses mixed with white lilies, tulips and so many other gorgeous, elegant blooms, I'm speechless. There's a table set with a tower of little pastries, stacks of pancakes and plates adorned with fruits. Candles of all shapes and sizes cover the floor of the gazebo.

I feel a knot in my throat because I just can't believe what is happening. Kit looks gorgeous in black trousers and a white button-down rolled up at the sleeves. He seems to have taken a quick shower and his hair is slicked back, revealing his every stunning feature. And right now, his expression is tight, nervous. And I know that I'm not dreaming, that this is really happening.

Heart thumping so hard I'm afraid it'll burst, I gulp and walk toward him. He has a bouquet of black roses in his hands.

I tell my feet to keep moving on the mirrored path and I already feel my eyes watering. He's smiling at me, so much tenderness and adoration in his eyes that I see my surroundings blur even more.

I finally reach him and the only thing I can say is "Hi" in a tiny whisper.

He says "Hi" back and then says, "You found me."

I laugh and quickly nod my head. "Yes I did, thanks to your clues." I hold up the gold arrow and turn my eyebrow up in question at him. "This?"

He smiles and taps his chest, right below his heart. "Taken straight from here," he says in the deepest, sexiest voice I've ever heard.

My vision blurs again and he says, "Alexandra… Shhh, baby, listen."

I wipe the stray tear from my cheek and see him kneel. Down. At my feet.

He takes my hand in his own and brushes a kiss over my knuckles. He meets my stunned gaze, his jaw clenching with emotion, his eyes fierce with it.

My heart constricts in my chest, and the tears start falling freely.

"I can tell you how from the moment I saw you, I knew you were going to make my world fall apart. I can tell you how from the moment you looked into my eyes, I knew no other man on this earth could have you, because those eyes are mine. I can tell you how you didn't have to do much other than challenge my every word and action to make me fall head over heels in love with you. But you know that. And I know that." The sense of conviction in his words flow to me, giving me strength to stay on my feet. "What I felt for you the moment I met you is but a shadow of what I feel for you now, Alex. You have shattered every expectation I ever had of love. Of life. I can't remember life before loving you. And I never want to have to. My soul is eternally bound to yours, and it wants to stay there."

He looks at me, and the love I see in his eyes makes my heart soar like an oncoming wind just carried it. I'm already nodding yes.

"So, will you honor me with a future by your side? Alexandra, will you marry me?"

He holds up the bouquet of black roses, a gorgeous ring tied to them with a gold ribbon. The colors of Cupid's Arrow.

"Yes. Yes, I will." I choke out.

He takes my left hand and unwraps a ring from the stems before sliding it on my finger. It fits.

Perfectly.

The diamond is stunning. An emerald cut, the sharp lines reflecting every ray of light that hits it. It's breathtaking. And so is *he*.

I keep nodding "Yes" like an idiot and laugh from the happiness before falling on the ground with him and wrapping my arms around him. I never want to let go. He holds me tight, planting kisses all over my neck and face.

"I love you, Kit," I whisper into his ear.

He holds me tighter, telling me he loves me back. We kiss among the candles, huge canopies of flowers towering over us, cocooning us in the gazebo, as the sun rises and coats everything in a golden glaze.

I close my eyes and say thank you. Because I never expected this miracle, it was brought to me. I say thank you, to the universe, to all the good in the world, to love, to miracles. I say thank you for this man and for this love. The greatest gifts I have ever received.

* * * * *

If you liked Kit,
you're going to love his brother!
What will it take to tame him?
Don't miss William "Stone" Walker's story
by New York Times
and USA TODAY *bestselling author*
Katy Evans.

Coming August 2019
from Harlequin Desire.

#2653 NEED ME, COWBOY

Copper Ridge • by Maisey Yates

Unfairly labeled by his family's dark reputation, brooding rancher Levi Tucker is done playing by the rules. He demands a new mansion designed by famous architect Faith Grayson, an innocent beauty he would only corrupt...but he *must* have her.

#2654 WILD RIDE RANCHER

Texas Cattleman's Club: Houston • by Maureen Child

Rancher Liam Morrow doesn't trust rich beauty Chloe Hemsworth *or* want to deal with her new business. But when they're trapped by a flash flood, heated debates turn into a wild affair. For the next two weeks, can she prove him wrong without falling for him?

#2655 TEMPORARY TO TEMPTED

The Bachelor Pact • by Jessica Lemmon

Andrea *really* regrets bribing a hot stranger to be her fake wedding date... especially because he's her new boss! But Gage offers a deal: he'll do it in exchange for her not quitting. As long as love isn't involved, he's game...except he can't resist her!

#2656 HIS FOR ONE NIGHT

First Family of Rodeo • by Sarah M. Anderson

When a surprise reunion leads to a one-night stand with Nashville sweetheart Brooke, Flash wants to turn one night into more... But when the rodeo star learns she's been hiding his child, can he trust her, especially when he's made big mistakes of his own?

#2657 ENGAGING THE ENEMY

The Bourbon Brothers • by Reese Ryan

Sexy Parker Abbott wants *more* of her family's land? Kayleigh Jemison refuses—unless he pays double *and* plays her fake boyfriend to trick her ex. Money is no problem, but can he afford desiring the beautiful woman who hates everything his family represents?

#2658 VENGEFUL VOWS

Marriage at First Sight • by Yvonne Lindsay

Peyton wants revenge on Galen's family. And she'll get it through an arranged marriage between them. But Galen is not what she expected, and soon she's sharing his bed and his life...until secrets come to light that will change everything!

HDCNM0319

SPECIAL EXCERPT FROM

HARLEQUIN

Desire

*Unfairly labeled by his family's dark reputation,
brooding rancher Levi Tucker is done playing by the
rules. He demands a new mansion designed by famous
architect Faith Grayson, an innocent beauty he would
only corrupt...but he* must *have her.*

Read on for a sneak peek at
Need Me, Cowboy
by New York Times *bestselling author Maisey Yates!*

Faith had designed buildings that had changed skylines,
and she'd done homes for the rich and the famous.

Levi Tucker was something else. He was infamous.

The self-made millionaire who had spent the past five
years in prison and was now digging his way back...

He wanted her. And yeah, it interested her.

She let out a long, slow breath as she rounded the
final curve on the mountain driveway, the vacant lot
coming into view. But it wasn't the lot, or the scenery
surrounding it, that stood out in her vision first and
foremost. No, it was the man, with his hands shoved
into the pockets of his battered jeans, worn cowboy
boots on his feet. He had on a black T-shirt, in spite of
the morning chill, and a black cowboy hat was pressed
firmly on his head.

She had researched him, obviously. She knew what he looked like, but she supposed she hadn't had a sense of…the scale of him.

Strange, because she was usually pretty good at picking up on those kinds of things in photographs.

And yet, she had not been able to accurately form a picture of the man in her mind. And when she got out of the car, she was struck by the way he seemed to fill this vast, empty space.

That also didn't make any sense.

He was big. Over six feet and with broad shoulders, but he didn't fill this space. Not literally.

But she could feel his presence as soon as the cold air wrapped itself around her body upon exiting the car.

And when his ice-blue eyes connected with hers, she drew in a breath. She was certain he filled her lungs, too.

Because that air no longer felt cold. It felt hot. Impossibly so.

Because those blue eyes burned with something.

Rage. Anger.

Not at her—in fact, his expression seemed almost friendly.

But there was something simmering beneath the surface…and it had touched her already.

Don't miss what happens next!
Need Me, Cowboy
by New York Times *bestselling author Maisey Yates.*

Available April 2019 wherever
Harlequin® Desire books and ebooks are sold.

www.Harlequin.com

Want to give in to temptation with
steamy tales of irresistible desire?

Check out **Harlequin® Presents®**,
Harlequin® Desire and
Harlequin® Kimani™ Romance books!

New books available every month!

CONNECT WITH US AT:

Facebook.com/groups/HarlequinConnection

 Facebook.com/HarlequinBooks

 Twitter.com/HarlequinBooks

 Instagram.com/HarlequinBooks

 Pinterest.com/HarlequinBooks

ReaderService.com

**ROMANCE WHEN
YOU NEED IT**

PGENRE2018

Love Harlequin romance?

DISCOVER.

Be the first to find out about promotions, news and exclusive content!

Facebook.com/HarlequinBooks

Twitter.com/HarlequinBooks

Instagram.com/HarlequinBooks

Pinterest.com/HarlequinBooks

ReaderService.com

EXPLORE.

Sign up for the Harlequin e-newsletter and download a free book from any series at **TryHarlequin.com.**

CONNECT.

Join our Harlequin community to share your thoughts and connect with other romance readers!
Facebook.com/groups/HarlequinConnection

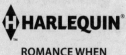

HARLEQUIN®

**ROMANCE WHEN
YOU NEED IT**

HSOCIAL2018

THE WORLD IS BETTER WITH

Romance

Harlequin has everything from contemporary, passionate and heartwarming to suspenseful and inspirational stories.

Whatever your mood, we have a romance just for you!

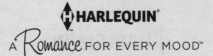